# MISADVENTURES WITH A SPEED DEMON

BY
CHELLE BLISS

# MISADVENTURES WITH A SPEED DEMON

BY
CHELLE BLISS

This book is an original publication of Waterhouse Press.


Cover Design by Waterhouse Press.
Cover images: Shutterstock



PRINTED IN THE UNITED STATES OF AMERICA

ISBN: 978-1-64263-002-2

*Meredith — Thank you for always being there for me.*
*You make me feel like the impossible is possible.*
*— Chelle*

# PROLOGUE

## BROOKS

"Drivers, start your engines!"

The crowd behind me cheers wildly and rises to their feet when they hear the magic words. I dig the tips of my tattered tennis shoes into the dirt and peer over the railing, standing on my toes to get a better look. I stare across the track as the cars roar to life, wondering what it would feel like to wrap my hands around the steering wheel and pump the gas, revving an engine just like they are.

Tyler, my mom's current boyfriend, smacks my shoulder. "Here's ten bucks. Get yourself something to eat, and stay out of my hair until the race is over," he says, thrusting a wad of money in my face.

I snatch the crumpled bills from his fingertips and shove the cash into my pocket. "Okay," I say with a shrug as he wanders away.

Tyler is a gambler, and every Friday while I watch the races, he places bets with the local bookies, trying to make enough to keep a roof over our heads for another week. He's been dating my mother for six months, which is longer than most men have stuck around. But I know soon we'll be on our own again because no one can put up with my mother for too long. If I had my choice, I would run away and never look back. Whenever Tyler gives me money, I stash it in a sock I hide in the vent in my bedroom, saving for the moment I can finally gain my freedom.

I tighten my grip on the metal railing and hold my breath as the flag waves and the cars take off. I live for Friday nights at the track. They're the only thing I look forward to anymore. There's nothing like the smell of burning rubber mixed with exhaust fumes, the stars twinkling overhead as the cars speed around and crash into each other before spinning out in a cloud of smoke.

I can't take my eyes off the track. I bounce on my toes, excitement coursing through my system as they get closer to the turn. My insides vibrate as the ground beneath my feet shakes from the rumble of the passing cars. There's no feeling in the world better than this, and I can't wipe the silly grin off my face.

I'm so into the race that I barely feel the tap on my shoulder until it happens again. I roll my eyes and turn my head, knowing exactly who is interrupting the race before I even look.

"Baby," she mouths, her voice muted by the noise around us.

My stomach drops at the sight of my mother. Her hair is matted down on one side and plastered against her cheek... probably held there by dried vomit. She smiles when my eyes meet hers, and I try not to stare at the mascara running down her cheeks, smeared in a way that looks more like war paint than makeup. Her torn T-shirt hangs off her shoulder, exposing her bra strap and probably earning her more than a few passing glances from the men around us. *God.* Why does she have to be such a mess?

"What?" I yell, but she can't hear me. I can't even hear myself over the cars whizzing by.

She says something I can't quite make out and sways, almost falling over. She wraps her hands around the railing next to me to steady herself, and I inch my fingers away. I glance around and pray no one from school is in the grandstands, seeing my mom so drunk she can't even stand up straight.

My body jerks forward as she yanks at my pants pocket. I know what she wants... What she always wants—the few bucks Tyler gave me, so she can buy herself more alcohol. I step back and swat her hands away without an ounce of remorse. That money is mine. Tyler gave it to me to buy myself something to eat. Not to hand over to her to buy herself more booze or drugs, because that's what she does with every penny she gets her hands on.

She narrows her eyes and moves toward me, yelling "*little fucker*," something she's called me my entire life. That's my mother. Not an ounce of love in her system for me unless I'm delivering a new bottle from the corner store she's too plastered to walk to. That's the only time she seems to like me anymore.

I turn my back and run through the crowd, weaving through what seems like an endless sea of people, without looking to see if she's following me. I know she's too drunk to stand without help, let alone run. I don't dare stop moving until I'm on the opposite end of the track, too far for her to make it in her current state.

By the time I find a new spot and look at the jumbotron, I've thankfully only missed ten laps. I assume the same position, my toes in the dirt near the fence, my arms against the railing, and my chin on top of my hands.

Monday is the first day of school. I'll officially be a freshman and one step closer to getting out of this shithole town and away from my mother. Someday I'll know how it feels to hug each turn with a car rattling underneath me, the freedom that comes with the racer life, and I'll never look back.

# CHAPTER ONE

## FAITH

"Why are we listening to this song again?" I stick my index fingers in my ears to block out the music that sounds more like small animals dying than an actual song. "It's obnoxious."

"Shut your face. This is a classic." Roscoe passes a car doing the speed limit, which is never acceptable in his book. He doesn't even bat an eyelash as the guy flips him the middle finger and screams out the window. "This is how I start every season."

I don't know why I agreed to let Roscoe pick me up this morning. I've never liked the way he drives, especially so close to the start of a new season. Even on the side streets, he thinks he's in a competition, dodging and weaving his way around cars like a maniac. Then there's his choice in music, which is sketchy at best.

"You know 'Highway to the Danger Zone' is about being a fighter pilot, not a race car driver, right?"

"Same shit." He shrugs and purses his lips.

Only my brother would equate speeding around in circles with something as heroic as a military fighter pilot. "You're a real dumbass, Roscoe."

"You love me, though." He glances at me with his lips turned up and his brown eyes twinkling. He waits for affirmation because he's a needy son of a bitch and always has been.

"Always." I tell him exactly what he wants to hear because he'd badger me until I did anyway.

He swerves around another car, and I grab on to the door handle, holding on for dear life. "What the hell is your hurry?"

"I'm warming up for the new kid," he replies quickly, and his cocky smile returns.

*Ahhh, the new guy*. I don't know much about him besides the few scouting reports my father slid across my desk a few days ago. What I've read has been nothing short of impressive. He's won over thirty titles and has become a champion on the smallest dirt tracks around the country. Not to mention he's amassed a small army of fans as well. My internet searches turned up a few photos but not much else, which was disappointing. I'd like to know more about the man who's about to become part of our team. I want to know what we're dealing with.

At the end of last season, my father decided it was time to expand and become the new unstoppable powerhouse on the race circuit. Roscoe balked at the idea. But my father didn't listen to Roscoe's whining and spent a month touring small tracks around the country, searching for the perfect match for our team. As soon as he saw Brooks Carter, my father jumped at the chance to sign a champion in the making to Ridley Racing.

Roscoe was livid that my father didn't consult him before

offering Brooks the full backing of our company. Roscoe never liked competition. Even as a little boy, he would throw a temper tantrum when he lost during our weekly family game night. He became such a killjoy, we finally switched from games to movies because he couldn't handle defeat.

Why on earth he became a driver in one of the most competitive sports, I will never understand. I always thought guys who raced were made of steel, like my father, but that was my mistake. My dad was a born leader and always in control, while Roscoe, well... He had winning down pat, especially with the help of my father and the entire pit crew at Ridley Racing. But even now when he loses a race, he goes dark and everyone ignores him for a solid week. He's unbearable at times, but he's the only brother I have...even if he can be a total asshole. There's no person in the world who knows more about me than Roscoe. He's always been there for me. When I was a little girl he was always at my side and never shooed me away like many of my friends' brothers did. We were like two peas in a pod for most of our lives, at least until he became a professional race car driver. Even now, we're on the road together half the year and often spend our downtime hanging out and relaxing because no one gets us better than each other.

"Do you know much about the new guy?" I ask as the track comes into view, shining in the distance from the morning sun. A surge of excitement fills me as we get closer. The new Ridley Racing is bigger, badder, and better than ever before, and I couldn't be happier seeing where our dad's dream is leading us.

"Just that he's a hotshot. I'm going to bring him down a peg or two."

Roscoe could be describing himself. For the last few years Roscoe has become a force to be reckoned with, and there is not a driver out there who doesn't want to knock him flat on his ass. Every rookie gets behind the wheel with victory in their eyes and Roscoe as their number one target. Each year, new drivers try to find their footing among the more seasoned veterans like my brother and ultimately fail, but their confidence somehow remains intact. I don't get it, but I guess it's all part of the racer mentality and something I'm never meant to understand.

"That's all you know? Did you even try to find out about him?"

"Nope," he says in a clipped tone.

I'm not surprised he has not bothered to do his homework. Why would he? He's the champion and thinks he's going to be on top forever. My brother no doubt believes there is no way Brooks has any hope of ever defeating him. He's Roscoe Ridley after all. Heir to the Ridley estate and bred from race car royalty.

"He's younger. About your age. He tore up the dirt tracks around the country, winning every major title, but that is not difficult on *that* type of track," Roscoe says.

*Typical Roscoe.* Nothing is as impressive as the professional circuit, and even then, he is never too impressed with anyone but himself. It doesn't matter what someone has accomplished; in his mind, no one can be better than him.

"Well, that's something. He must be good if Daddy wants to bring him on board." I try to bring him back to reality a little bit before he walks into this meeting with guns blazing, shooting off at the mouth like he typically does.

"He had a spot to fill, and no one else was available. It's just that simple," he tells me, but we both know he's full of shit.

My father doesn't do simple. He researches, runs the numbers, and does more research before finally making a decision. He'd never settle on just anyone to fill a spot unless he thought the person was worthy, capable of winning, and would bring glory to our family name.

"You know that is not true. They'd line up around the building for a shot to race on our team." I motion toward the small crowd that has already assembled outside the entrance to prove my point. "See?"

Roscoe adjusts in his seat, straightens his back, and leans over the steering wheel, clearly annoyed by my statement. "No one wants to compete with me, Faith. You need to understand that."

I roll my eyes and groan. "You're so cocky."

"I have to be."

My brother's self-confidence, as annoying as it is, derives from the fact that he is the reigning champion. No one has piled up more wins during the exhaustingly long season than he has. He has basically ruled the field with the help of my father and the amazing pit crew without any real competition. I wonder if that is about to change.

I wave to the familiar faces of the diehard fans as we drive by, reading their handmade signs welcoming Roscoe back for another season.

"It's my name on those signs," he says to drive his point home. "Do you know why?"

"Because they don't know what an asshole you really

are?" I snort, but Roscoe doesn't find me the least bit funny.

"Because I'm *the* champion."

Half of the crowd gathered outside the track are women, and I'm pretty sure most of them don't care if he wins the next race. They're just hoping to land in his bed with the delusion of becoming Mrs. Roscoe Ridley.

My brother, for all his faults, is a good man and handsome as the devil too. Women fill the grandstands each weekend dressed head to toe in Roscoe Ridley official gear. Sales of female clothing alone are well into the millions—almost outselling our male clothing line. Unlike me, Roscoe has my father's dark-brown hair, brown eyes, and tanned skin. Women want him because he is good-looking, just like my dad.

When we finally pull onto the infield, my father's standing near the edge of the track, surrounded by a small group of Ridley Racing employees.

"Pop looks happy," Roscoe says with his lips turned up.

My father's wearing his lucky shirt, the same one he wears every year when he first steps foot on the track. The Hawaiian shirt is covered in a hideous pattern from the seventies, but he refuses to throw the damn thing out. The faded palm trees on the front are bad enough, but the pink flamingos are the icing on the cake. Somehow, he pulls it off. My father stands tall and proud, his back perfectly straight and his shoulders pushed back as he talks to the man next to him. My father laughs and smooths down the salt-n-pepper hair of his beard. The stress of last season has vanished from the corners of his eyes, replaced with a glow I haven't seen before.

I cover my mouth and hide my smile to avoid aggravating

Roscoe any more than he already is. “He does look happy, but he’s always excited at the start of a new season,” I remind him with a sideways glance.

Roscoe parks his truck near my father’s before cutting the engine. “It’s a dog-eat-dog world out there, and no one’s going to beat me.” He ticks his chin toward the crowd and snarls. “Not even that kid.” My eyes follow his and land on the back of a man just as tall as my father but with a more sleek and slender frame.

I open the door and step onto the running board of Roscoe’s ridiculously tall monster truck, trying not to fall on my face from the uneven grass. “That’s some bullshit,” I mumble, knowing he’ll be dethroned eventually.

Roscoe jumps out and quickly rounds the back of the truck to confront me. “What did you say?”

“I said that’s the truth.” I lie through my teeth because I already know this day is going to be a shit show. One of two things is going to happen: Roscoe will either show his dominance and leave the track happy, or Brooks Carter will put on a display that’ll have Roscoe lunging at the boy’s throat.

His shoulders relax, totally buying my lie. “That’s what I thought you said.”

Roscoe doesn’t even know what dog-eat-dog means. He was handed a full sponsorship the day he told my father he wanted to follow in his footsteps. Roscoe didn’t have to fight his way onto the track like so many others. As the son of a racing legend, he had a winning team behind him from the moment he asked. And the fact that our family is one of the wealthiest in Buxton means he didn’t have to bus tables to pay rent while he proved himself worthy of sponsorship. He was literally handed his dream career along with a hefty paycheck.

My father walks in our direction, stroking his beard, and his smile causes the balls of his cheeks to almost touch his eyes. "There's my girl," he says with his arms outstretched, waiting for me.

Roscoe grumbles as I curl into my father's arms, and he wraps me in a tight embrace. My brother practically looms over us, waiting for my father's attention, but I've always been the favorite. He would never admit that, especially not in front of my brother, but he has told me many times. Then again, I'm sure my dad told Roscoe the same damn thing about himself because that's the type of man he is...always a peacemaker.

"Hey, Daddy." I squeeze him tightly, wrapping my hands around his middle and interlocking my fingers behind his back until my face smashes against his broad chest.

My father's lips graze my cheek as he pulls away, tickling me with his beard. "Looking beautiful as always, Faith."

I grin up at him, basking in his compliment like I always do, and tighten my arms around his middle.

"I love you, pumpkin," he says before glancing over my shoulder at Roscoe, who's mumbling something about me being a suck-up.

Roscoe pushes me to the side with the back of his hand as soon as I move away from my dad. "Hey, Dad," he says, stepping between my father and me.

"Son." My father gives him a quick hug followed by a pat on the back before breaking all contact. "We have a long season ahead of us, but it's going to be the best one yet."

"Best ever," Roscoe says as we follow my dad toward the waiting race cars, but there's no excitement in his voice like there usually is.

"I want you two to be nice to Brooks. He's going to bring something different to our team."

"Sure, Daddy," I say, earning an easy smile from my father, but Roscoe remains silent.

"Brooks," my dad calls out, draping his arms around our shoulders as he pulls us closer to his sides like a proud papa. "Brooks, I'd like you to meet my kids."

Brooks Carter steps forward from the crowd with his broad shoulders and piercing blue eyes. The photos I dug up did not do the man justice. Damn, he is handsome. Dare I say the most handsome man about to take the field this season. I glance down for a moment, avoiding his penetrating gaze.

"Kids, this is Brooks Carter." My father tightens his grip when Roscoe and I don't say anything right away.

I lift my gaze, meeting his, and attempt to swallow the lump lodged in my throat but fail.

"Hey," Brooks replies when I still don't speak.

My stomach flutters uncontrollably as Brooks's gaze sweeps down my body. The wind is knocked out of me for a moment. I do nothing but stand there like a mute idiot and gawk. His full lips, blue eyes, and tanned skin complete the well-built package and have rendered me dumb. Even with the shabby tattered clothes, he's hot as hell.

"Hi," I barely squeak out. My voice already cracked on the one syllable, and I didn't trust myself to say anything else without sounding fifteen again.

Roscoe thrusts his hand between us, staring at Brooks and breaking the awkward moment. "Roscoe Ridley," he says.

Brooks slowly drags his gaze from mine to focus on my brother, the real star of the family. "It's an honor to meet you, sir."

*Oh Lord.* The respect Brooks shows to Roscoe is not lost on any of us, especially my brother. Feeding into his ego is dangerous in the long run but completely effective in the short term.

Roscoe's chest puffs out a little more than usual as Brooks slides his palm against my brother's. "My father tells me you're a champion in your own right." That's Roscoe lingo for *you're not as important as me,* and Brooks knows it.

My eyes widen, but thankfully no one's looking at me. They're too busy with their staring contest mingled with their ego fest.

"I've crushed dirt tracks all over the country, and I'm here to do the same." Brooks smiles, unaffected by Roscoe's shit talk.

The imaginary ego gauntlet has officially been thrown. They haven't even climbed into their cars yet, and the silent war is already brewing.

Roscoe holds his stomach and laughs like it's the most absurd thing he's ever heard. "That so?"

"Why else would your father bring me here?" Brooks doesn't even so much as blink.

Brooks and Roscoe stare each other down, silently appraising one another, and the tension in the air multiplies. They are acting like little boys on the playground, not like men who are supposed to be part of the same team.

It takes all of one minute for the gloves to come off and the ego fest to grow into an out-of-control shit storm. I would not even be the least bit surprised if they each whipped out their manhood to see whose is bigger. Ego is something I don't find attractive. Swagger, yes. But when a man's ego gets in the way of reality...I have issues. I've spent my entire life around race car drivers. I know exactly what they are all about. There is not a more egotistical group of people on the planet. They're adrenaline junkies, notorious hotheads, and they're sexist as hell. They have more in common with cavemen than civilized society.

My father steps between them, sensing the growing unease. "Now, boys." He runs his fingers through his short gray hair and lets out a small sigh. "Let's remember we're all on the same team here." My dad doesn't realize there is no hope for these two. I can see it from where I'm standing, but somehow, he doesn't. "This year is about team domination and not just about personal accomplishments," Dad adds.

Roscoe will never accept Brooks. Never. Brooks will always be an interloper, trying to take over Roscoe's spot at the top. No matter how well Brooks drives, he'll never be good enough in Roscoe's eyes. Lord forbid he unseats Roscoe as the champion; our family will never be the same.

"Faith," Dad says. I know that tone. He's about to ask me to do something he knows I don't want to do. I can tell by the way he says my name.

"I'm going to have you spend some time with Brooks and show him the ropes." My eyes flutter to Brooks's as my dad keeps talking. "Roscoe has enough to do with the season fast approaching. I don't want to take away from his training and preparation. So, I'm leaving Brooks in your capable hands."

Roscoe's close to the edge of having an all-out meltdown because the new kid may be a real contender. A very *hot* contender too. One who oozes sex and could quite possibly take away Roscoe's title as the hottest driver on and off the track.

Brooks is staring at me with those fierce blue eyes, grinning from ear-to-ear as I nervously twist my hands together in front of me. "Sure, Daddy. Whatever you need."

Roscoe growls and cracks his knuckles, clearly not happy with the entire situation. As my dad walks away with his arm slung around Brooks's shoulder, Roscoe leans over and whispers, "He's not one of us, Faith. Remember that."

I peer up at Roscoe and roll my eyes—something I find myself doing often because he's a jerk. "Seriously. You need to get a grip. He is one of us."

If I don't help Brooks, who would? Brooks is officially a member of Ridley Racing, which means it's my job to make him feel comfortable and help him settle in so he's completely focused on winning when the season starts. I love my brother, and I want him to be the champion, but I'll do anything to make Ridley Racing bigger and better, even if that includes becoming the official welcome wagon—against my brother's wishes.

"Faith!" my dad yells from a few feet away when he realizes I've fallen behind and am still standing at Roscoe's side.

"Coming," I call out. I stalk away from my brother with a

small smirk on my face because I know Roscoe is finally about to find out what dog-eat-dog means.

Unlike Roscoe, I wasn't given my position in the company. Instead, I attended Vanderbilt University, double majoring in business and marketing. Yeah, I could've asked my father for a job, and he would've gladly handed it over after I graduated high school, but that's not what I wanted.

I worked my ass off so I could someday become the head of the company. Roscoe never bothered to learn anything more than what was absolutely necessary. Plus, everyone knew he wasn't smart enough to handle the day-to-day operations. I wasn't even convinced Roscoe could count higher than ten. To him, complex math was anything he could not add on his fingers.

Brooks keeps his eyes on me as I walk to where he's standing with my father. Why does he have to be so damn good-looking? The look on his face is one I've seen before and has the butterflies coming back to life.

"Let's have Brooks and Roscoe take a few laps so they can get a feel for how the other drives."

"Sure thing," I say, staring at Brooks with a giant smile.

My dad clears his throat, drawing my attention away from the pretty boy and earning me a curious look. "I'm going to talk to Roscoe for a moment. Will you show Brooks to his car?"

Roscoe's kicking the grass under his feet, staring up at the sky, and cursing. My father heads toward him as I turn around and practically faceplant into Brooks's chest. The man is like a solid wall of muscle without an ounce of softness.

I stumble backward and reach out, trying to latch on

to something...anything to stop myself from falling. Brooks reaches out and catches me, but I quickly find my footing and straighten.

"Easy there," he says in the sweetest Southern drawl as his hands slide across the skin of my arms.

I straighten my back and finally find my footing along with my sanity. *He's just another man.* No one has ever rendered me stupid with a simple smile, but somehow Brooks Carter has that effect on me. I don't like it either. "Thanks," I say, pulling away from him. Even as I stalk toward his waiting car, I can still feel his hands on my skin, like he'd scorched my flesh with his touch.

"Thanks for this," Brooks says as he jogs to catch up with my long, confident strides.

"It's my job, and I'm happy to do it," I say as I gaze up at him with heated cheeks.

"This track is impressive," Brooks says with an adorable lopsided grin.

I train my sights on the car just a dozen feet away and not at the handsome man at my side. "It is." I say nothing more, preferring to stick to the task at hand. Brooks needs to get in the car and show us what all the fuss is about. He may have conquered the dirt, but driving on asphalt is an entirely different experience.

"I really do appreciate your help."

I turn my head and look at him briefly, praying my embarrassment from running into him and my unwelcome attraction to him isn't written all over my face. "It's really not a problem, Brooks. You're one of us now."

His eyes linger on my lips, doing nothing to calm my inner butterflies. “I like the sound of that, but I haven’t earned my spot yet.” The corners of his mouth turn up into the most drop-dead gorgeous smile.

I take longer strides than before, picking up the pace to stop myself from saying something awkward and embarrassing myself even more. I’ve never been this flustered around a man before, but there’s something about Brooks Carter that has me off-kilter. I don’t know if it’s his good looks, cocky smile, or the fact that I haven’t been with a man in months, but my body is totally into him.

Trying to play it cool, I drape my arm across the roof and slap the shiny, newly polished, cobalt-blue paint. “We want you to get a feel for her today.” I peer down, unable to stop myself from checking out his ass in his well-worn and tight-fitting jeans.

He rests his arms on the window frame and leans inside. “She’s a beauty,” he says as he turns his face toward me, catching me checking out his ass.

I snap my gaze away from his bottom and curse under my breath, chastising myself for being a complete idiot and getting caught in the process. “Don’t go wild out there. See how she suits you.”

“Wild?” He lets out a short, sexy laugh, which slides into a wicked grin. “I’m always in control, princess. Always.”

My face turns ten shades of red when he winks, and I finger my necklace, sliding the pendant back and forth in short, jerky movements while I ignore his statement. “We’ll make modifications to help you be as successful as possible before the first race."

"Are we just about ready?" my dad calls out as Roscoe slides into his car.

Brooks straightens, claps his hands together, and pins me with his eyes. "Let's get it on!"

I'm in so much fucking trouble.

# CHAPTER TWO

## BROOKS

I'm not even out of the car before Roscoe Ridley is in my face, howling like a maniac with his arms waving wildly in the air. I keep my mouth shut and let him express his anger. The sting of me beating him in front of his father, sister, and employees has to be brutal, but it was necessary. I figure now is as good a time as any for him to get used to seeing my bumper in front of him.

"You're a reckless asshole." He thrusts his hands against my chest as soon as my feet touch the asphalt. "You could've ruined my car."

I toss my helmet onto the seat behind me and shake my head. This isn't really how I wanted the day to turn out, especially not with Roscoe and me getting into a physical altercation within the first hour. But I'll stand my ground. I'm not his little brother, and he needs to learn that I'm his equal on the track. I may not have the same trophies lining some fancy mantel like he does, but my own wins are no less impressive. I refuse to let Roscoe treat me like some low-life drifter off the street.

"My job is to drive this car and to be the best damn driver on the course. That's what I did out there." I cross my arms in front of my chest and keep my cool. I've dealt with people like Roscoe my entire life. Between school yard fights and bar room brawls, some asshole always felt the need to start some shit to make himself feel better.

I beat him almost every lap around the track. Sure, I let him start off strong, allowing him to get comfortable before I took my chance and pulled ahead. Before I stepped foot in Georgia, I spent countless hours studying his race tapes and learned his every move. He has weaknesses, and I plan to exploit every single one of them to my advantage.

"You showed no control." He is practically foaming at the mouth with anger as he speaks. "You're a typical rookie."

I raise an eyebrow. "I had enough control to overtake you." He charges toward me with his fist pulled back, and I prepare for the punch, widening my stance, ready to dodge and weave before he can connect.

Unable to hear our heated exchange, Mr. Ridley claps as he walks in our direction. "That was superb," he says, stopping Roscoe's hand in midair. "I couldn't ask for anything more."

Faith stands behind her father, staring at me over his shoulder with a look I can't quite place.

"Thank you, sir." I flicker my gaze from Mr. Ridley to Faith.

"It was all right," Faith says with a shrug like she's not impressed by my stellar performance. "Could've been better."

Roscoe turns toward his father and points at him. "That's how you want him to drive? Have you gone mad?"

Mr. Ridley tucks his thumbs in his waistband and rocks back on his heels. "Boy, that's exactly how I want him to drive."

Roscoe growls and throws his helmet across the track in a full-blown temper tantrum. "I can't deal with this. I'll meet you back at the office."

Mr. Ridley waves his hand toward Roscoe as he stalks away. "Don't mind him. He'll come around eventually."

I have a feeling that *eventually* will never come.

Roscoe's hatred for me is real, and I would probably feel the exact same way if I were in his shoes. Maybe I shouldn't have gone after him so hard, but this isn't a sport for sissies. He was being an asshole, and I couldn't stop myself because he would do the same damn thing if roles were reversed. I know damn well if I ever want to earn his respect, I have to do it on the track.

"We better get going, Daddy. We shouldn't leave Roscoe alone too long." Faith glances in my direction, but she looks away quickly. "Brooks can follow us."

Mr. Ridley touches Faith on the shoulder, staring down at her in a way no one has ever looked at me. "Why don't you ride with Brooks, sweetheart? Get to know each other a little better. You're going to be spending a lot of time together, and I'd like him to feel at home here."

Feel at home. I'm not even sure what that's supposed to mean. The closest I've ever come to feeling at home anywhere is inside the beaten-down trailer I bought off another driver when I started touring the dirt tracks around the country. It isn't much, and it sure as hell isn't pretty, but it is mine, and no one can take it away from me.

She sighs as her shoulders sag forward. "Fine."

So far, I haven't received much love from anyone other

than Mr. Ridley, but I never thought this would be easy. To expect anything different would have been disastrous for my psyche. I did not come here to make friends. I accepted a position with Ridley Racing to cut my teeth in this business and find a spot on the circuit.

Mr. Ridley motions toward our trucks and glances at me and then Faith. "Let's get this show on the road. Shall we?"

Faith walks at her father's side while I follow closely behind. The rhythmic sway of Faith's ass has my full attention. It's not a casual walk but is filled with class and oozes femininity. I imagine she has been a good girl her entire life, falling in step with whatever her daddy wanted.

I don't blame her either. If I had Mr. Ridley as my dad, I probably would've been a goody-two-shoes too. Instead, I'm stuck with a mother who is who knows where. I get random texts from old friends that she's been spotted and is still alive. I tried to save her life more than once. I tried to get her into rehab, but she didn't want to change. Every time I got her off the streets and sober, she always found her way back to her first love, which lay at the bottom of a bottle.

Roscoe Ridley is a fool for not understanding what a lucky bastard he's been. He has a loving father and a sweet sister and all the money a guy could ever need. He grew up with a silver spoon in his mouth, never had to worry about a goddamn thing. He was handed a racing empire just because he was born into the right family.

He did not have to claw his way to the top.

He does not know what it is like to be hungry.

I do, and I am starving.

## FAITH

Even with music playing on the radio, the silence between Brooks and me is damn near deafening and completely uncomfortable. We've barely spoken five words to each other since we left the field, walking toward the Ridley headquarters.

I turn toward him, ready to say something, but immediately clamp my mouth shut when I can't think of something funny or charming to say. Brooks stares at the road ahead, oblivious to my gaze as he taps his thumb against the steering wheel to the beat of an old country tune.

Brooks has a tiny bump near the ridge of his nose I hadn't noticed before. I imagine he got it from one too many fights. He's a hothead, just like every driver I've ever known, including my brother. Roscoe would have a bump in the same spot if it hadn't been for my mother's insistence that he see the family doctor and have his nose set to avoid plastic surgery in the future.

"Are you a big city kind of guy?" I cringe a little but hide it with an uneasy smile. I don't even know why I asked such a stupid question. The way Brooks dresses doesn't scream slick city guy in any way, but I couldn't take the silence anymore, and it was the first thing that popped into my head.

"Mountain man," he replies, taking his eyes off the road for a second and glancing in my direction.

Those damn butterflies flutter around my insides again like crazed little Brooks fans. Flashes of a sweaty and shirtless Brooks chopping wood play like a naughty movie reel on a constant loop. The vision of his perfectly tan, dirty body glistening in the sun from a hard day's work has my mouth watering.

I turn my attention toward the window, trying to push the sexy images of Brooks out of my head to stop myself from drooling. "Sounds like hard work and completely exhausting."

"I love getting my hands dirty. I've never been one for the bright lights of the big city. Hopefully someday I'll own a ranch and settle down with nothing but mountains as my company. You?"

"I grew up a few miles away, but I'm sure you did your research."

"Yeah, but I didn't learn much about you or your mother."

"Oh." I glance in his direction and find his eyes on me and not the road. "Eyes," I say, pointing toward the windshield and grabbing my chest with my other hand. Then it hits me. Brooks just admitted he tried to find information on me but failed.

*Interesting.*

"Sorry." He tightens his grip on the steering wheel and leans forward, giving the road his full attention. "Tell me something about Faith Ridley."

"What do you want to know?"

"Everything."

My face flushes. "Man, the sun's hot today." I fan myself with one hand and roll down the window with the other. The cabin of his truck seems to suddenly feel stifling. "There's not much to tell. I attended Vanderbilt University and graduated with honors. Now I work for Ridley Racing."

"You just told me what you do, not who you are."

I reach for the pendant around my neck, sliding the

diamond from side to side. "I'm a country girl at heart..."

"Stop," he says, interrupting me from finishing my boring monologue about who I am. "What's one thing about Faith that would shock me?"

I bite my bottom lip, turning his words over in my head, but come up empty. "I'm really a boring person."

His eyes twinkle as he looks in my direction. "I find that hard to believe."

I really am boring, even if he doesn't want to believe me. Growing up as a member of the Ridley family, I had to behave or I'd land on the front page of the local gossip rag. That was the problem with growing up in a small town. Nothing stayed private for long.

It's one reason I went to Vanderbilt. I needed my freedom and a break from Buxton. I thought I'd love the city life, but I quickly learned that when the bright lights and decadence wore off, any city just becomes a bigger version of Buxton.

I can feel his eyes on me. "A bunch of us are going out later for drinks. We're celebrating the start of the season."

"That's cool."

I fidget with the hem of my skirt. "Want to come?"

Why did I ask him that? *Because he's hot.* If I'm being honest with myself, Brooks Carter, for all his ego, is the hottest man to cross my path in a very long time. I promised myself I'd never date a race car driver, but that didn't mean I couldn't invite him for drinks. Maybe he'd feel more at home and would make my job a little easier.

"Hell, yeah. Thanks."

"You're welcome."

Brooks's eyes grow wide when he catches his first sight of our headquarters. The two-story office building with a giant attached garage could easily fit twenty cars if my father decides to expand even more. When Roscoe told him he wanted to follow in his footsteps, my father could not have been prouder, and Ridley Racing was born. My dad has built an empire in a short amount of time, and the entire thing revolves around his past career and growing another legend in the family. We pull into the half-full lot and park next to my father.

"Damn. This place is impressive." Brooks leans forward, mouth hanging open as he stares up at the building.

"Wait until you see inside."

He shakes his head as he leans back and takes it all in. "I've never seen anything like it."

"Expect to have your mind blown, Mr. Carter."

"Brooks, please," he corrects me, tilting his head back and grinning.

Everything about Brooks is sexy, not just his easy smile and beautiful blue eyes. I'd seen hundreds of races in my life, but not one of them had me squeezing my thighs together like today's practice did. I held my breath every time he hugged the inside of the track or tapped my brother's bumper, waiting for him to spin out. He commanded the field, always in control just like he'd stated before he climbed into the front seat and pulled onto the track.

Maybe I had Brooks pegged all wrong. I assumed he was an egomaniac like Roscoe, but the man opening my door to help me down from his truck seems to be nothing but a gentleman. When I place my hand against his palm, my fingers itch to touch the rest of him. He leans forward, and for a moment, I hold my breath, thinking he is going to kiss me.

"You kids coming?" my dad asks, breaking whatever moment we were having.

I shake my head and pull my hand back as soon as my feet touch the ground, scurrying toward my father and averting certain disaster.

# CHAPTER THREE

## BROOKS

Faith has had four shots of tequila along with a few beers, matching me drink-for-drink just as she promised before we walked into the bar. Roscoe didn't bother to show up, but no one seemed to care about his absence, especially me. The rest of the group has already called it a night, probably because Faith and I are pretty much shitfaced drunk and verging on obnoxious.

"You're not the best at everything," Faith says right before she hiccups and covers her mouth. Her eyes go wide, and she giggles softly behind her hand before another hiccup bubbles out of her.

The prim and proper woman of earlier is gone, replaced by a carefree and fun country girl. God, she's so freaking beautiful, with her pink cheeks and pouty mouth complete with lush, kissable lips. Everything about the woman drives me wild and has the blood coursing through my veins faster than I can drive around any track, even at breakneck speed. I know she's technically my boss, but that doesn't stop me from having all sorts of dirty and inappropriate thoughts about her.

"How would you know?" I raise an eyebrow, teasing her

from across the table.

"Well, I..." She drags her hands down her cheeks. "I'm drunk," she slurs as she tries to set her elbow on the table and almost misses. She giggles again, but this time it's somehow louder than before. Her eyes flutter closed as she places her face against her palm and sways.

I bribed the waitress with an extra twenty bucks if she'd leave the bottle at our table and give us a little privacy for the rest of the evening. I wanted Faith's complete and undivided attention. I pour myself another drink but don't refill her glass. I think she's hit her limit, whether she wants to admit it or not. I can't allow her to drink any more. "You're holding your own, but I think it's time to call it quits," I tell her when her body finally stills, and she opens her eyes again.

"I'm not a quitter." She narrows her gaze, going almost cross-eyed in the process. When she reaches across the table for the bottle of tequila, I snatch it away from her reach. "Give it to me," she snaps, and then reaches for it, wiggling her fingers.

My cock twitches in my pants, and I shift in my seat but don't dare give her the bottle. "Come on, princess. We all have our limits, and you've hit yours."

"Brooks." She smiles lazily and leans forward with her breasts on top of the table. I can't drag my eyes away. No matter how much I want to look anywhere else, it's like she has me in some teenage trance. "I'm a grown woman."

"I know." My voice is almost a whisper. I don't realize I'm still staring at her breasts until her fingers push against the tequila bottle. I snap my gaze away from her well-endowed cleavage and find her smiling at me. "There's nothing you can do to change my mind."

"Nothing?" She slides her tongue across her bottom lip, and my eyes follow.

*Fuck.* How did Faith Ridley, the good girl who still calls her father "Daddy," suddenly become the woman across the table taunting me with her breasts and beautiful mouth for another shot of tequila? It doesn't matter because the fact that my dick is stirring in my pants, begging to be freed, tells me I approve even if I shouldn't.

"Nothing." What a crock of shit. The word doesn't even come out of my mouth sounding convincing.

She shifts in her seat and then drags the wooden chair close.

In response, I move the bottle again, still keeping it far enough away for her not to reach. "Tell me something about yourself like I asked earlier, and maybe I'll give you another."

I'm still lying. I won't give her another drink. The last thing I need is Faith passed out so I have to explain to her father why I let her get so out of control—in public no less. I'm sure word would get back to him. In a town this small, nothing stays hidden for long, no matter how hard people may try to bury it.

Faith finally pulls her hand back but keeps her chest on full display "Well"—she glances around the bar before smiling—"I kissed a girl once."

I cough, almost swallowing my tongue with that confession. "What? When?" I have so many questions I can't seem to speak fast enough. I lean forward and push my cock down, reminding the damn thing I am in control. "How did that happen?"

"I was a freshman, and it was pledge week. That's all you need to know." Her smile widens, the corners of her mouth almost reaching her deep-green eyes as she pushes her glass toward me.

I lift the bottle and shake it. This is dangerous territory and I know it, but I can't stop myself from pushing her for more.

She leans back and brushes her auburn hair back over her shoulder. "Fine. I had to kiss Katie McGee for sixty seconds."

"Where?"

"On the mouth."

"No." I laugh. "I mean, where were you?"

"Oh." She giggles and blinks. "We were in the living room of our sorority house."

I shake my head, jealous of anyone who was in that room that night. "To be a fly on that wall," I whisper.

"What?"

"Nothing."

"What about you?"

"I've kissed a girl on the mouth too." I smirk and wiggle my eyebrows, trying to make light of the situation because my pulse has already sped up like I was running a marathon.

She laughs loudly and slaps her hand across her mouth when it turns into a snort. "You're an asshole."

"I know."

She leans over the table, scanning the room once again. "Have you kissed a boy?" she asks in a hushed tone.

"Nope." I'm not the least bit sorry to disappoint her. Kissing another dude with their facial hair tickling my lips has never been on my to-do list. There isn't a damn thing in the world that would make me want to place my lips on another man's.

"That's sad." She frowns like she just heard the saddest news in the world. "You don't know what you're missing."

I tilt my head to the side. "You're a funny chick, Faith."

"No really." Her eyes brighten, and she bobs her head. "Kissing a girl was okay, but there's nothing like a man's touch as his lips slide across yours and the stubble of his chin brushes against your skin."

I wave her off, needing her to stop. "Nope. Not for me." I easily brush off the thought of kissing a man, because I can't stop picturing kissing Faith. I want to reach across the table, place my hand on the side of her face as I lean in for a kiss. I can almost taste the shiny lip gloss she reapplied three times in the last hour as I dip my tongue between her lips.

"So, you're saying you're one hundred percent into chicks?" When my head jerks back, Faith giggles uncontrollably. "Your face," she says, pointing at me as my mouth hangs open still in shock that she is questioning my manhood.

"You got some jokes, li'l girl. A smart mouth too."

"No. For real, though." Faith places her hand on top of mine, stroking her thumb across my skin. "I may need proof."

*Shit.* This is all kinds of bad. She's drunk and so am I, but I know we're treading in dangerous water, and I'm not sure I have the power to pull myself free from the Faith Ridley riptide.

I growl, almost at the breaking point, and the tequila is doing nothing to make this situation any easier. "We better get out of here before you pass out," I say, but I really mean before I do something I can't take back and will cause a bigger headache tomorrow than we're probably both going to have already.

"You can't drive like this," she says, swaying as she tries to stand up from her chair.

I reach out and wrap my hands around her upper arms to steady her. She glances up, her eyes meeting mine, and the invisible electricity in the air crackles. My heart races, pounding in my chest uncontrollably as I stare into her green eyes. "I'll call a cab for us. It's really not a big deal."

Faith places her hand against my chest, scorching my skin through my T-shirt. "We're in the middle of nowhere. There are no cabs." Her fingers crumple around my T-shirt, fisting it tightly as she gazes at me with glassy eyes. "My place is just around the corner, though." When I don't reply, her hands slide up to my shoulder before landing on my biceps. "Come on. I'll be a good girl. I promise." She grins.

My palms start to sweat, and my dick presses against my jeans as if reaching for her warmth. "I don't think it's a good idea, Faith."

"Don't be a prude." She squeezes my bicep and lets out a little throaty moan as we step outside. "I live in a loft and have plenty of room. If something happened to you tonight because you're drunk, my daddy would kill me." She pouts, making it impossible for me to say no.

I am more afraid of her father killing me if he finds out I spent the night at his daughter's place than I am of hitching a ride back to my trailer and being murdered by a stranger. I already have one Ridley hating me, and the thought of another makes my stomach turn.

"Don't be a baby, Brooks. It's the responsible thing to do."

And because I've had four shots of tequila and I'm not thinking clearly, I say, "I'll sleep on the couch, and I'll be out before you're awake." Even drunk, I know I should walk my ass back to my trailer to avoid being alone with her, but I can't bring myself to say the words.

Right now, with her hands on my skin, almost in my embrace, with her sweet-smelling perfume swirling around me, there's nothing I want more than more time with Faith.

"Don't worry about that." She rests her forehead against my shoulder, still squeezing my biceps. "No one will see you. I promise."

"But I'm sleeping on the couch." I repeat that phrase like somehow it makes the entire situation more acceptable.

"Sure." She giggles and sways again as she tries to straighten after finally releasing my arms.

"Steady there, princess." I wrap my arm around her waist and pull her against my side. "I think you overdid it tonight, and we're going to pay the price tomorrow."

She peers up at me with a lazy smile. "Maybe just a little, but it was worth it."

"Let's get you home and into bed."

She bats her eye lashes. "Why, Brooks. How very forward of you."

*Fuck*. This could be bad. No, this could be horrible and the dumbest thing I've ever done. And I've done a lot of stupid things in my day.

We stumble toward Faith's place, laughing and holding

on to each other for support. I don't realize how drunk I really am until I collapse on her couch after she disappears into the bathroom. I lift my head, trying to focus in the haze of white and pink that surrounds me. The amount of lace and furry shit in her place is mind boggling. Who needs ten throw pillows on the couch in every shade of cotton candy pink?

Faith's loft is huge. I don't know why I figured her place would be a normal-sized apartment. Instead the damn thing takes up half of the top floor and has no walls except for the bathroom. There will be nothing separating us tonight besides a couple dozen barrier-free feet of space.

"You okay in there?" I lift one of the pillows, close my eyes, and inhale. I groan into the pillow, smashing it against my face and clutch the edges tightly in my fist as Faith's perfume washes over me. My dick stirs. I'm torturing myself, making the entire situation worse.

"I'm fine," she calls back. "Just make yourself comfortable."

I toss the pillow to the side before pulling off my shirt and grabbing a nearby pink blanket. The room starts to spin as I lie back and stare at the ceiling. Between wearing my jeans, my dick having a mind of its own, and Faith being so near, sleeping is going to be impossible.

## FAITH

After I slip into something a little more comfortable and a lot more revealing, I carefully pad across the floor, making a detour toward the couch on the way to my bed. My gaze is fixed on Brooks's bare, moonlit chest beckoning me like a beacon in the darkness. His rock-hard body calls to me in a silent tease, and my fingers itch to touch him. In a moment of weakness, I lower myself down next to him. He doesn't stir as the couch dips from my weight. With the alcohol coursing through my system, my mind is fuzzy, but the one thing I know for sure is I like Brooks.

More than I should like a man I barely know. More than I should like an employee. The simple fact that I haven't been with a man in any way for over a year doesn't make my ability to stop fantasizing about Brooks any easier.

"Brooks," I whisper, watching him carefully for any sign of consciousness. Brooks's chest steadily rises and falls as his eyes remain closed, but he doesn't stir. I reach my hand out and gently touch him, careful not to wake him up. For a second, I think he's passed out, and I sweep the pads of my fingers across the most luxurious hardened silk of his flesh.

Just as I am about to pull away, he wraps his hand around my wrist. I freeze as my gaze snaps to his face, connecting with his piercing blue eyes. "What are you doing, princess?" His voice is hoarse and needy.

"I don't know," I admit but do nothing to retract my hand as my fingertips hover over his chest, trapped by his grip. We stare at each other with only the sound of our breathing filling the large open space.

"You're playing in dangerous territory." He sweeps his tongue across his bottom lip.

I focus on his mouth, watching the slow drag of his tongue. My insides flutter as if I'm in a trance. "I know."

"You need to go to sleep." His grip tightens, throwing me mixed signals and confusing me.

"Brooks," I whisper and squeeze my legs together, trying to calm the ache. "We can't do this."

"I know."

Neither of us move. We stare at each other as the air around us crackles as if some invisible force field is holding us together. My pulse quickens, and my breathing becomes more labored.

"It's been so long since anyone's touched me." The words come out easy. Too easy. "Maybe you should kiss me so we can get whatever this is out of our systems." The tequila logic totally works for me. I mean, that could work—a single kiss could kill the attraction I've felt since the moment I laid eyes on him.

Marcus, my last boyfriend, was an awful kisser. I should've known we would never last, but I really liked the guy and tried to get over my kissing hang-up. I figured in time, he'd get better, but it never happened. The day I caught him banging my sorority sister, giving her the sloppy kisses I thought were reserved just for me, wasn't the easiest pill to swallow but made ending the pointless relationship easier. Maybe Brooks kisses worse than Marcus... It could totally happen.

Brooks lets out a shaky breath and glances toward the ceiling. "So dangerous," he says into the darkness.

"I won't tell if you don't." I smirk. "Plus, it may be the worst kiss ever."

He pins me with his eyes, and all the air rushes from my lungs. "Princess, I'm a damn good kisser." His fingers relax around my wrist as an easy smile plays on his lips.

I bite the side of my bottom lip as the couch dips when

Brooks shuffles closer. "You sure you want to do this?" He places his hand above my hip, and I shiver from his touch.

"Yes." My voice shakes on the single syllable, craving more.

He shifts but never breaks contact, keeping his hand on my hip as he faces me. "Come here," he says, tugging on my hip and pulling me toward him.

The delicate butterflies from earlier are back and bouncing off my insides as I climb into his lap. Our eyes are locked as I settle against the hard bulge in his jeans and lean forward, sending tiny sparks throughout my system at the contact.

"Just a kiss," I say, splaying my hands against his rock-hard chest and loving the soft warmth of his skin against mine.

"Just a kiss." He nods slowly as he flickers his gaze to my mouth. One arm snakes around my back as I lean forward, hovering my lips near his. "Only one."

My heartbeat thunders in my chest as he pulls me closer. This is it. The moment of truth. I hold my breath, waiting for his lips to touch mine as I practically squirm against him. He tightens his grip on my hip, stopping the slow slide of my pussy against his cock. I start to pull away, but Brooks slides his hand up my back and leans forward, sealing any doubt I had with his lips. There is nothing sweet about this kiss as he grips the nape of my neck.

I let out a tiny sigh and breathe again before losing myself in the kiss. Our tongues tangle in a haphazard and desperate dance of lust. I push my fingertips into his chest and squeeze my thighs against his hips, pressing my core against his thick shaft.

I am desperate with need and overcome with greed as I rock against his cock. The roughness of his palms as his hand gropes my ass sends ripples of pleasure down my spine. Unable to control myself, I pick up the pace, grinding against him rougher than before.

Firmly holding my neck with one hand and my ass with the other, he pulls his lips away. "Slow down, Faith."

"I want you," I moan and stare down at him, filled with so much pent-up energy that I want to tear his jeans off and ride his hard-on until I pass out.

His lips cover mine again, stifling every moan that reverberates from the back of my throat. My body shudders when his hand slides between my thighs and brushes against me from behind. Raising my core from his jeans, I push my ass toward his hand, wanting more of him.

So much time has passed since I was touched by anyone other than myself, I almost forgot how much pleasure a man's touch could give.

"So. Wet." Brooks moans against my lips when he presses his fingers against my opening.

My body is practically shaking with want. I ache to be filled and consumed by the rock-hard man beneath me. When his finger finally pushes inside, I clamp down, relishing the feel of him inside me.

"Fuck me," I whisper against his lips as I push my bottom out farther to give him better access. I want to be stretched out in order to lessen the throb Brooks has caused between my legs.

"I'll fuck you in time, princess. I want to feel your beautiful pussy come against my fingers."

I buck against his rough palm, pushing his long finger deeper. He answers my silent plea and presses another thick finger inside, making my insides rejoice with pleasure. My entire body quakes as he pulls his fingers out and plunges them back inside. Leaning forward, I press my clit against the coarse denim of his jeans and the only thing that separates his cock from me.

I rock backward, fucking myself against his hand as he curls his fingers inside and drives me closer to the edge. Our motions are smooth and seamless, like we have done this a million times before. He hits the right spots and never misses a stroke, even when I pick up my pace, grinding my clit against him feverously.

I'm so close to orgasm that I dig my fingers into his chest, grounding myself to him. My insides tighten around his fingers as I slam my body against his wide digits that are working me like a master.

He pulls my face closer, swallowing every sound that comes from my throat and grows louder the closer I come to that long-awaited orgasm. With a harder, deeper thrust of his fingers, my body coils, and pleasure rockets through my system. I can't breathe. My body spasms, and colors explode behind my eyelids.

I tremble against his chest, and my arms shake. I try to hold myself upright through the frenzy. His lips never leave mine, feeding me air when my lungs cease to work.

When I pull my face away, I glance down at the man lying under me. His lips are fuller, red from the kiss, but filled with more hunger than before. I gasp for air, trying to regain my composure as my body jolts with aftershocks.

My hardened nipples poke through the delicate fabric and scrape against his chest. Brooks doesn't say a word as he sits up, and his fingers ease out of my wetness. Our bodies stay connected. Even after an amazing orgasm, I want more.

He leans forward, cradling my back in his hands as he lays me down on the couch. Covering my body with his, he places his lips against my neck and kisses my tender flesh. I reach between us, fumbling with his zipper because I want nothing more between us. I still crave to be filled by him and to watch his face as he comes inside me.

My breath hitches when his mouth covers my nipple, tonguing me through my teddy. I work faster, tearing at his jeans and using my feet to push the fabric down his legs.

"I need you," I say when his cock springs free and spills between my legs. When he doesn't move his hips fast enough, I dig my heels into his ass and push him against me. "Fuck me."

He lifts his head, peering down at me through the darkness with turbulent eyes. "Maybe we..."

I seal his lips in a kiss and palm his cock in my hand, stroking the hard length so the tip bumps against my wetness. He moans with pleasure, closing his eyes as he moves his hips toward my opening.

As the head of his cock pushes into me, I wrap my legs around his waist and arch my back to give him full access. I want every bit of his length inside me.

Our kiss becomes more frenzied, and his strokes become more targeted. He rears back and slams into me, stealing my breath. I tangle my fingers into his hair and drag my nails against his scalp as he thrusts inside. There is a deliciousness to the pounding. The relentless pursuit of his pleasure pushes me toward another orgasm.

No man has ever given me two. Not until Brooks Carter. I push the thought away. This is a one-time thing, scratching our itch and getting need out of our system so we can work together for the season. It's a shame he is so skilled with his cock and he's an employee, because I could get used to pleasure like this.

He slows for a moment, grinding his hips and moving his cock inside me without pulling out. Whatever he's doing causes my mouth to go slack and all thought to vanish.

I push my head into the couch cushion, letting Brooks control the movement and pace as our lips devour each other. I could lie like this all night and be fucked by him.

A few seconds later, the slow assault of his hips changes, his movements quickening with urgency. He slams into me, pounding my clit with every thrust and sending me right over the edge. This orgasm is different than the first and much more intense.

My toes curl, and I am unable to stop my eyes from rolling back as pleasure crashes over me. Brooks follows, grunting as he collapses on top of me. I gasp for air as our sweat-covered bodies stick together, and I realize I've made a mistake.

# CHAPTER FOUR

## BROOKS

My eyes snap open, and I turn my face toward the soft snores echoing across the room. *I slept with Faith Ridley.* I sling my arm over my head, softly cursing under my breath. What the hell was I thinking? Obviously, I wasn't.

Too much tequila didn't help my decision-making process either. I had the hots for Faith from the moment she strolled across the infield with her fire-red hair, deep-green eyes, and slamming curves. I knew I should've gone home when the rest of the crew left the bar, but Faith convinced me to stay. In all honesty, I wanted to be alone with her.

The damage has been done. There is no going back after what we did last night. No take backs are allowed after sex, and no amount of alcohol can wipe away the memories. I can't undo what happened, but I have to learn to roll with my colossal mistake.

I've barely slept since she tip-toed to her bed, leaving me naked and wanting more. Instead, I have been chastising myself for being the biggest asshole on the planet. I know better than to sleep with the owner's daughter—or any woman who's drunk, for that matter. I have done some stupid bonehead shit in my life, but this has to take the cake.

My entire career is on the line, and my cock led me astray. I think back to the way she touched me, groping at my chest as I tried to ignore her. I should have stayed still and pretended to be asleep, but I couldn't. I tried. God, how I tried to keep my dick in my pants, but when I peered up at her wearing nothing but that skimpy teddy, I lost my ability to think with anything other than my dick.

"Are you awake?" Faith whispers from across the room.

I scrub my hand down my face, feeling more trouble coming on. For a moment, I toss around the idea of not answering her. If I were smart, I would pretend to be asleep, but once again, I am not thinking with a clear head. "Yeah." I glance at the clock and realize it's almost four in the morning, and in just a few hours, I'll have to walk into work, pretending this never happened.

"Come here."

I push myself up and grab my jeans off the floor before moving toward her. I should keep my ass on the couch, because going to her while she is naked in her bed is not a smart move. But based on the events that have already occurred, why should I bother thinking clearly now?

"Leave the pants there," she says.

I immediately drop them.

Stalking toward her with nothing covering my body, my cock swinging and growing harder with each step, I promise myself something. I won't sleep with her again. I shouldn't, at least. I am human after all. She moves the blanket and pats the mattress next to her. She's gorgeous in the faint glow of the street lights sprawled across her bed with only that damn teddy covering her body.

"Sit," she orders.

I slide onto the bed next to her and follow her eyes as they dip to my cock.

"That needed to happen. I needed to get you out of my system." She gives me an uneasy smile.

My body rocks backward. I have never had a girl sleep with me as a means to an end. Or at least they never openly said the words, but Faith is different. The same thought floated through my head as my fingers pushed inside her sweet pussy. It was a lie I told myself even though I knew it was complete bullshit.

She isn't a one-night stand I can just forget. I will be spending months with her on the road. Her tits and ass will follow me, and resisting her will be damn near impossible.

"I don't know if I can say you're out of my system now, princess." Based on the reaction of my body, getting a taste of her did not scratch an imaginable itch but unleashed something in me I sure as hell hadn't expected.

She rolls to her side, her gaze sliding to my cock every few seconds. "Will you sleep with me?"

"Again?" I raise an eyebrow. I'm up for the challenge. My dick has always risen to the occasion and has never let me down. Why would tonight be any different?

*It is just your entire life on the line...idiot.*

I stay where I am with my cock safely between my legs—feet away from any of her meaningful parts.

"It's been a while since I've cuddled with someone."

I should've known she'd be a cuddler. No chick has so much girlie shit with fur and lace everywhere without wanting to tangle her body around mine. Cuddling sounds so innocent, but I know keeping my hands to myself isn't going to be easy. "So, no sex?"

She grabs my arm and pulls me toward her. "Come on. Hold me."

I'm thinking with my dick again as I slide under the covers. My brain is telling me to run and get the hell out of there, but then my skin touches hers, and all reason flies right out the window.

She curls her body in the crook of my arm like this is the most natural position in the world. Her fingers trace a pattern across my chest as she stares up at me. "Are we going to be able to work together after this?"

I don't know how to answer the question. Faith has the power to get my ass booted off the team and sent back to the dirt track, but that's the last thing I want. "I think so. I can be an adult."

I don't say another word. What else is there to say after what we just did? We're both in a difficult spot. She is the owner's daughter. I haven't even been in town forty-eight hours, and I have already made every damn mistake possible.

Her fingernails dig into my chest. "Brooks."

"Yeah."

"I like you."

"I like you too," I admit.

"I shouldn't like you, though."

I peer down at her deep-green eyes and smile. "Why?"

"You're nothing but trouble."

I pull her body closer and rest my hand over hers. "You're not the easiest person either, Ms. Ridley."

"I need to hate you. It will make this so much easier."

"Yeah," I mumble against her forehead and close my eyes. I know I'm in trouble. The feelings she's stirred in me are already one hundred times more powerful than anything I've ever felt before.

Faith Ridley has crawled under my skin, surrounded me in her scent, and I'm afraid there's no escape.

## FAITH

My head's pounding as I rub my temples and try to focus on my father's words after he's been at it for two hours. He keeps tapping his finger against the whiteboard, but the massive hangover I have makes it sound like he's punching the damn thing. The tequila aftermath is making it damn near impossible for me to listen or digest a single word my dad's saying. Then there's Brooks. He's barely made eye contact with me since we sat down and is acting like last night never happened. The bastard.

How does someone even do that? I can put on an act and pretend like everything is business as usual in front of other people, but he hasn't so much as given me a sideways glance or a sly smirk. Sure, he said hello when he walked into the building...but that wasn't much after he rolled out of my place before dawn without so much as a goodbye.

What a goddamn fool I'd been. I tasted the man. I know how he sounds when he comes and the funny face he makes too. In all my dumbass, alcohol-buzzed glory...I really thought sleeping with Brooks would be a good thing. I scratched the proverbial itch, thinking I'd get him out of my system, but it seems to have done the opposite.

I glare across the table at Brooks and resist the urge to sigh again. My dad's already given me more than one strange look. I'm trying to maintain my usual chipper attitude, but I'm failing miserably. My stomach's in knots, both from the lingering tequila and the cold shoulder Brooks is giving me, but I plaster a fake smile on my face anyway.

As Dad rolls into the numbers from last season, I tune him out. I prepared the report and know the details better than anyone in the room. I can't stop staring at Brooks, and I'm pretty sure everyone in the room has noticed besides my father and maybe Brooks because he still hasn't bothered to make eye contact.

I'm practically seething by the time my father walks behind me, creating a shadow across the table. I place my hand over the notepad I'd been scribbling on, covering Brooks's name in the center of my doodle. I still, praying to God he didn't see anything I had on the pad before I tried to conceal it like I was a kid in high school being caught by the teacher.

"Let's break for lunch and dig back in this afternoon. Sound good with everyone?"

I quickly grab the pad of paper and tuck it against my chest before climbing to my feet. "Lunch sounds great. I'll be in my office if anyone needs me."

Dad clears his throat and places his hand on my shoulder before I have a chance to walk away. "I thought we could all go together."

Those were not the words I wanted to hear. By all, I assume he means the four of us. We can't possibly leave Brooks, the new golden boy, out of the equation. Sitting across from him the last few hours has been horrendous, but at least I could play it off like I was deep in work mode. But lunch... That would be an entirely different situation, and I hate the very idea of sitting across from him while our feet touch under the table.

Roscoe grumbles, clearly disliking the idea as much as I do.

"I don't want to put anyone out," Brooks adds from across the table and finally looks in my direction without so much as a smile of acknowledgment. "I'm more than happy to..."

"Oh no." Dad puts his hand up and stops Brooks from continuing. "We're a team, and we're going to start acting like one." My dad's heart is in the right place, but he has no idea what he's saying or what happened last night. Thank God.

"Sure, Daddy." I plaster on a wide and very fake smile.

"Fine," Roscoe growls and climbs to his feet. "We can be a team, but it doesn't mean I have to be best friends with the man."

I glance toward Brooks, who's rubbing the back of his neck with a forced, uncomfortable smile, and I almost feel bad for him. Yesterday, I would've felt awful, but that was before Brooks Carter laid his hands on me and stole my breath with a single kiss. The fact that we slept together wasn't my issue, but his inability to acknowledge my presence besides a quick look doesn't sit well with me.

I'm so sick of Roscoe and Brooks's bullshit. I'm ready

to pop. The headache climbing up my neck and gripping my temples like a vise isn't making it easy for me to keep my cool. I place a hand on my hip, still clutching the notepad, and spout off. "Stop acting like a baby, Roscoe. You're still the champ, and maybe you should act like it. Brooks beat you a few laps. It's not the end of the world." Roscoe gawks at me, blinking a few times like he's in shock. I've always been on Roscoe's side, even when I knew his ass was wrong, because he was my brother, and that's the type of shit siblings do. "If you're so worried you're going to lose to him, maybe you should just concede the entire season now," I add, rubbing salt into his wounded ego.

Roscoe slams his hands down on the table. "You're such a little bitch sometimes, Faith." He flares his nostrils and bunches his shoulders up near his head, but I haven't seen that type of fire in his eyes in a long time. "I'm not conceding this season, and *that* boy"—he points at Brooks, who's still sitting at the table, stunned—"is *not* going to beat me."

My father slides his arm around Roscoe's shoulder and gives him that manly, father-son squeeze. "I'm starving, kids. I think you're all just hangry and need to fill your bellies with some good food."

The room is silent, and my eyes drift to Roscoe, who's staring at me in confusion. We both turn our gaze to my dad because the man has never uttered the word hangry in his life. He's not one to be up on the "young kid lingo," as he says.

"Have you been watching YouTube again, Dad?" Roscoe asks, finally breaking the weird silence and relaxing under my father's touch.

"I saw something on the internet and thought it was funny.

It fits you, my boy. When you get hungry, you're sure an angry little beast."

I chuckle at my father's characterization of my brother. It's spot-on. Roscoe has always been a baby when he's hungry. His entire teen years were unbearable, and if I didn't know any better I would've thought he was pregnant because of his nonstop grazing in the kitchen. He wasn't happy unless he was cruising around the track or stuffing his face until he could barely walk.

"I want barbeque for lunch," Roscoe announces as he turns his gaze toward Brooks. "If I have to sit with Brooks, I at least want to eat something good."

I wince, tensing at his shitty statement. Everything out of his mouth today is god-awful, and by the way my dad's eyes narrowed, Roscoe is about to get his ass chewed out.

"Faith, take Brooks down to the Tasty Pig, and I'll ride with Roscoe. He and I need to have a little chat alone."

Roscoe looks to me for rescue, but I give him no reprieve. He deserves everything that's coming to him. Sure, he doesn't like Brooks. Neither do I at the moment, but that doesn't give him the right to be an all-out asshole to him in front of my father. Even if my father hated someone, he always smiled and did his best to remain a good Southern gentleman, which was something Roscoe never mastered, no matter how hard my father tried to teach him. Roscoe is in for it. A little chat with Daddy is never a good thing. Roscoe knows he stepped over the line, and he's about to get straightened out.

I walk ahead of Brooks, ignoring him as he follows me to the truck. I stash my notebook in my purse, climb inside his truck, and slam the door, feeling a little bit of satisfaction after taking it out on his vehicle. "You need directions?" I ask as he slides in next to me.

"I saw the Tasty Pig on the way in this morning. I think I can find it again."

We sit in silence as he pulls onto the main road. I fidget with my purse, riffling through the contents to find my lip gloss. I glance at him under my eyelashes and stare at his hand resting near his knee. He's leaning back, calm, with one hand on the wheel, relaxed into the driver's seat of his pickup like nothing ever happened between us. I should keep my mouth shut and let it slide. I knew I was making a mistake by sleeping with a guy I barely knew, but I couldn't control myself.

"We have to talk," I say, unable to sit in silence any longer. On top of everything, neither of us stopped pawing at each other long enough to use protection. I'm on the pill, so there's no worry about having a mini Brooks making a surprise entrance in nine months, but that doesn't mean he didn't pass me some nasty STD he picked up from some racing groupie.

"I'm all ears."

I growl and curl my fingers into a tight fist, holding down my anger long enough to ask the most important question that's been burning on my mind. "When was the last time you were tested?"

"I'm clean, Faith. Don't worry about that."

*Don't worry about that?* That's not an answer. That's a cop out. At his quick dismissal, my anger rises from irritated to ready-to-burst in under three seconds.

"You did not answer my question, Brooks."

"I had a physical and full work-up last week. Everything came back clean. Relax a little. How about you? When was the last time you were tested?"

I jerk my head backward at the absurdity of the question. "Are you serious?"

"Don't act shocked. Why would you ask me that if I can't ask you? The question's fair, princess."

I cross my arms over my chest and try not to feel defensive. It is fair for him to ask, but that doesn't make it easier to swallow. "You've slept with way more people than me, Carter."

I've slept with exactly two people my entire life, and one of them is sitting next to me pretending the entire thing never happened. Marcus, my college boyfriend, was the other, and I made sure to get an STD test after I caught him fooling around. I thought I was safe with him since we were committed to one another, but man, I couldn't have been more wrong.

"To be honest, I haven't slept with anyone but you," he admits, glancing in my direction.

Now he's totally yanking my chain, and I'm not happy about where the conversation is going. I draw my eyebrows down and narrow my gaze on his baby blues. "You were *not* a virgin."

He laughs and shakes his head. "Of course not, but I haven't slept with anyone in a long time." He pauses and shifts in his seat. "Let me restate that. I really have never actually slept in a bed with anyone. Sex and sleeping are two different things. And for the record, I haven't had sex with another chick, besides you, in a long time. I'm totally clean. There's nothing to worry about."

I sit there, staring at him in disbelief, as I try to process what he's just said. He's fucked other women. Nothing shocking there. But it's the next part of his statement that has me hung up. He never slept with any of them. How is that even possible? I mean, everyone gets tired after sex. Don't they? Marcus always passed out immediately afterward like my vagina put some magical voodoo spell on him, and he couldn't keep his eyes open. But Brooks... He probably sneaked out of their beds just like he did mine.

I cross my arms over my chest, put a shitty smirk on my face, and decide it's time to just come right out and say it. "Sneaked out on them too, huh?"

"Easy, princess." He shakes his head and sighs. "For the record, I didn't sneak out."

"What do you call it, then? You were not there in the morning. No note. No text...nothing."

I'm pretty sure that's the very definition of sneaking out. He didn't even bother to wake me before he left. It shouldn't have mattered because we were nothing to each other. Not really. But somehow when he acted like I barely existed in the office, it hurt like a punch to my gut.

"I left before the sun came out because you know as well as I do word travels in a town like Buxton. Would you rather I stayed and your dad find out about it?" He glances in my direction, and I turn my face, hiding my heated cheeks at my complete stupidity over the entire situation.

"No. I don't want my daddy to know, but that doesn't explain why you ignored me all morning." I'm hurt and spent all morning letting my feelings get the better of me.

"Faith." There's softness to his voice. "I couldn't look at you."

My shoulders slump forward, and I swallow the bitter pill of reality that his words just delivered. "I get it." I lift my hands from my lap. "We're nothing to each other. I got the message loud and clear, Brooks."

This was exactly why my mamma told me to never sleep with a boy unless we were committed to each other. She explained a long time ago that was the difference between men and women. Sex draws our feelings to the surface, leaving an imprint on our hearts as well as our bodies. It's something we can't just toss to the side. Brooks is the first person I let past second base without being in some sort of meaningful relationship, and her words sure as hell are ringing true.

He rolls to a slow stop at the stoplight near the Tasty Pig. "Hey."

I don't answer him. I can feel his eyes on me, but I don't dare look. My vision blurs as tears line the bottom of my eyes. I'm not crying for some imaginary lost love. I'm embarrassed and upset because I was stupid enough to think he'd be different. I knew what I wanted last night to be, but somehow, when I woke up this morning, I thought it meant more to both of us.

"Faith," he says as the truck rolls forward through the green light and he turns into the parking lot.

I keep my eyes trained on the storefronts lining Main Street and blink back the tears. "Yeah?"

He pulls into the first open spot and cuts the engine. "Look at me."

I take a deep breath and replace the sadness with my best pissed-off glare before I face him. "What?" I bite out.

He shifts, leaning his back against the door to face me head on. "I couldn't go back to how things were. I couldn't talk to you like nothing happened."

"So you ignore me instead?" I let out a disgusted grunt. "Save it for one of the floozies who will buy your lines."

"Last night wasn't a quick casual fuck. When you walked in this morning, I couldn't pretend. I figured it was better to keep my head down and mouth shut before I got myself in a heap of trouble."

I blink and gawk, my mouth hanging open, as Brooks swipes a hand down his face and smacks his head back against the rear window of his truck.

"I could still smell you on my skin when I got home, and I couldn't stop thinking about the way you tasted and felt in my arms. I told myself it meant nothing, and I damn well had myself convinced until you came barreling through the garage with that killer skirt, just enough cleavage showing to drive me wild, and swaying your hips as if you were trying to torture the fuck out of me. Do you know how hard it was to not pull your ass into the parts room and have my way with you? I mean, can you imagine that shit show if someone would've caught us?"

"Oh," I say and swipe my fingers across my neck, feeling my pulse racing underneath. "I didn't..."

"You just assumed I'm an asshole."

"Well..." I'm speechless. I rarely have trouble finding words, but around Brooks, I seem to be at a loss more often than not. He keeps throwing curve balls, totally knocking me off-kilter with admissions that I'm not expecting.

"I didn't lie when I said I liked you, Faith. I like you way more than I should." He slides his hand across the seat, covering the top of my hand with his soft warmth. "I've worked so damn hard to get where I am now, and the entire thing could blow up in my face. In less than twenty-four hours, I've managed to do enough damage to ruin my entire career. I'm not used to feeling something for anyone."

"We sure made everything complicated in a hurry. Didn't we?"

"A mess," he replies with a small laugh as he squeezes my hand, "but a totally hot one."

My brother knocks on the window, and I jump, totally missing them pulling in next to us. "We better go," I say, reaching for the handle but leaving my other hand still under his. I don't want to break the connection or lose the moment we're having after such a horrible morning. I let my insecurities show, but Brooks doesn't seem to be holding it against me.

As I start to pull away, he tightens his grip on my hand. "You want to do it again sometime?"

My head snaps to the side, and my eyes widen for a moment before warmth fills me inside. "Yeah. I'd like that."

*What the hell am I doing?* I don't have time to take my answer back or pick apart my dumb response because Roscoe's standing at the hood of the truck, pointing at his stomach and hollering. Maybe having sex with Brooks while sober will be just what I need to get him completely out of my system. The tequila could've impaired my memory to the point that last night seemed like the best sex of my life, right? With any luck, the second time would definitely not be as spectacular or mind-blowing, and we'd both walk away sated with the most awkward start to a new friendship. Maybe.

There is something about Brooks Carter that has my brain scrambled. The shit's already hit the proverbial fan. The damage is done. Whether we do it once or twenty times won't matter in the eyes of my dad or Roscoe if they find out. We have already committed the sin, and I might as well get everything I can out of the man before the groupies get their hooks into him.

# CHAPTER FIVE

## BROOKS

Mr. Ridley has not stopped talking since we sat down at the Tasty Pig, and I'm soaking up every story he's telling about the good old days. The man is overly enthusiastic about everything, and it's infectious. In his day, he was the biggest name in racing, holding multiple championships and winning more races than anyone in history. Being across from him, listening to him talk about his life, is still surreal. I realize I haven't stopped staring at him, with my mouth probably gaping open like a starstruck kid the entire time.

I remember watching him on television and wishing I was the young boy standing at his side during the after-race celebration. That was Roscoe, the lucky prick. He was always there, sitting on his dad's shoulders, being paraded in front of cheering fans. I was so jealous of that damn kid, and part of me still is. Instead, I had a deadbeat mother and no father in sight. I wanted someone to scoop me into his arms and twirl me in a circle, showering me with so many kisses my cheeks would be wet. But that never happened.

Roscoe and Faith are the lucky ones. They were showered with love and affection, wanted for nothing, and never had to worry where they'd sleep each night. It's hard for me to wrap my head around the simple, easy life they had and took completely for granted.

Whatever Mr. Ridley said to Roscoe on the way here didn't seem to damper his hatred of me. He hasn't stopped glaring at me with his arms folded and his upper lip curled in disgust. I brush it off. Roscoe is just a spoiled asshole. Someday he and I will have it out, but that day won't be today.

Faith is sitting next to me. She is leaning forward with her elbow on the table and resting her chin in her palm. Her other hand is under the table on my leg.

I keep both of my hands fully in sight on the table and try to act as casual as possible as I hang on Mr. Ridley's every word.

"So, Brooks." Mr. Ridley finally pauses for the first time in the one-sided conversation.

"Yeah?" My voice cracks as Faith's hand slides higher up my leg.

"Your racing career is impeccable, but I want to know more about Brooks the man. I couldn't find much about your family. Do you mind filling in some blanks?"

This is the conversation I've always dreaded having. Explaining my past and my mother is something I've never grown comfortable with, no matter how many times I say the words. The pity always did me in. Sure, I wish shit would've been different, but that doesn't mean I want everyone to feel sorry for me either.

I push my empty plate forward as I ease back against the booth, staring straight ahead. "Not much to tell, sir. I didn't have much of a happy childhood." I can feel the mood around the table change as soon as the words leave my mouth.

Faith's grip tightens on my legs, and when I look at Roscoe, he's no longer glaring at me.

Mr. Ridley tosses his napkin on top of his plate and rests his hands on the table with a tense smile. "Family is something I take very seriously. I can't imagine what you went through, but I'd like to know more because it helped shape the man you are today. No matter how shitty it was, without it, you may not be sitting across from me today. I brought you into our family, making you one of us."

Faith's hand slides back near my knee, and the boner I was close to sporting a few moments ago vanishes. Talking about my shitty past is a surefire way to bring everything crashing back to reality and completely suck the pleasure out of any situation.

"Only for you, Mr. Ridley. It's not something I like to talk about, but like you said, it's made me the man I am today." I force a smile on my face and take a deep breath.

I know Faith's now hanging on my every word, her body still as she sits at my side. Roscoe stabs at the meat on his plate but keeps glancing in my direction. Maybe they need to hear my story. I wouldn't be here without my past. I'd probably be living on the beach, some boring-ass banker, soaking up the rays and banging some hot blonde with implants bigger than my head.

"My father ran off before I was born, and I've never met the man. Don't much care to, neither. We lived in a small town where everyone knew each other's business. My mom was an alcoholic. Usually drank our rent money, getting us tossed out of more shitty apartments and motels than I can remember. My favorite times were when she'd pass out on the couch, so I could watch television in peace without her calling me a *little fucker* for not fetching her more booze."

Mr. Ridley shakes his head, tightening his hands into fists. "That's a damn shame. I hate hearing that. Makes my blood boil. I'd lay down my life for my kids, and I can't imagine..." He stops and clears his throat. "I don't want to be rude. It's not nice for me to talk about your mamma."

"It's fine, Mr. Ridley. She wasn't really a mother except through birth. She did nothing for me. I see how you are with your kids. Even now, they're grown, and you shower them with more love than my mother ever showed me."

"Dude, that's awful." Roscoe drops his fork as he shakes his head and grunts. "I can't even imagine."

I wave my hand in the air, dismissing their sadness for me. "It sucked, but I'm over it. That's my past and not my life anymore. Or my future." I turn toward Faith, scared of seeing pity on her face more than anybody's right now.

There's no pity but maybe some sadness lingering near the corners of her eyes. But I see something else...understanding, possibly. "I'm so sorry, Brooks," Faith whispers.

No one wants bad shit for kids. They're the purest, most innocent creatures on the planet. It didn't matter how many times my mom called me names; I did nothing to deserve her hatred. In her book, my birth was probably the biggest mistake of her life, and she made sure I paid for that honor every single day.

“Did your mamma sober up eventually?” Mr. Ridley asks.

“No.”

His face tightens. “She still in your hometown?”

“Don’t know. Don’t care. I stopped talking to her a few years ago, sir.”

The words sound so harsh coming from my mouth. I mean, we’re supposed to love our mothers more than anything in the world, but she was supposed to love me first and failed at every turn. I could no longer pine for the person I wish she was and needed to leave her in the past where she belonged.

“What got you into racing?” Roscoe asks like he hadn’t been ready to rip my head off less than five minutes ago.

I let his earlier anger slide. I can be the bigger man, forgetting what happened before to move forward. I’ll do anything to be part of this team; hell, I’d give my left nut to be part of this family. Dealing with Roscoe was nothing compared to the bullshit my mother put me through. “Tyler, one of my mother’s boyfriends. He was a heavy gambler and used to take me to the track while he placed bets with the bookies. The first time I heard the rumble of the engines, I was hooked.”

“There is nothing like the sound of the engine and the car coming to life underneath me.” Roscoe grins, almost seeming friendly. “It’s a feeling I can never describe to anyone, but everything about it feels right.”

I’m almost dumbfounded as Roscoe carries on a regular conversation with me like we just met and the last twenty-four hours never happened. Yesterday, he wanted to tear my head off and stomp on the damn thing.

Mr. Ridley grips Roscoe’s shoulder and gives him a quick

nod. "I knew you were destined to be behind the wheel. When you were a baby, it was the only way I could get you to stop crying. Your mamma would beg me to take you for a drive. It's a damn good thing we lived in Buxton with the track down the street. The faster I drove, the quieter you were."

"I know, Dad. I've heard the story a million times."

"This one." Mr. Ridley motions toward Roscoe with his chin. "Always a pain in my ass, but I still love him."

I'm green with envy at the easiness of their relationship. I imagine they spent hours bent over the hood of a car, tinkering with the insides until each car was a fined-tuned beast. I wanted that more than anything. I saw my friends running home to spend time with their fathers after school while I did everything in my power to stay out of my mother's crosshairs.

"That man Tyler teach you how to drive too?"

I shake my head, wishing he'd stuck around long enough to teach me a damn thing. Just like every other man my mother got her hooks into, once she bled him dry, he took off and never looked back. "I taught myself at the beginning. After a while, one of the old-timers got sick of watching me mess up and took me under his wing, trying to teach me everything he knew. Bart Williams was the man's name, and I'll never forget the look on his face after I won my first race. I'd never seen someone so proud of me. He stood at my side, arm draped over my shoulder, and smiled like he'd just crossed under the checkered flag instead of me. When Bart died from a sudden heart attack on the floor of the garage, I decided it was time to move on and try my hand at the dirt circuit. I'd try my best to make the man proud and make all his hard work mean something."

"You are, kid, and he did damn good." Mr. Ridley nods with an easy smile. "You may not know it yet, but you were born to be a champion."

I shift in my seat, my gaze moving between Roscoe and Mr. Ridley, and I don't dare look at Faith. The compliments and kindness coming from everyone, especially Mr. Ridley, are almost too much for me to handle all at once. "I don't know if I was born a champion, but I'm trying damn hard to make it my reality."

"The first race is in a week. You'll cut your teeth there, and we'll see what happens. You have to earn your spot in the main race, but you have a damn good shot."

"I'll make you proud, sir."

I want to win, but more than anything I want to make him proud, just like I did Bart.

"I have no doubt, Brooks. You've already impressed the hell out of me." He turns to Roscoe and gives him a lighthearted slap on the back. "Roscoe too. It's why he's so cranky. You remind him too much of himself. All balls-to-the-wall cocky and filled with hunger."

"Something like that," Roscoe says while chewing his last piece of barbeque chicken. "Then there's the fact that you're an asshole." Roscoe flinches as Mr. Ridley reaches for the check, but I can't imagine his father ever laying a hand on him.

"I need everyone at the house tonight at seven," Mr. Ridley states as he studies the tiny slip of paper. "It's our annual charity ball, and Faith has busted her hump this year. The wealthiest people in the town will be in attendance, so be on your best behavior or you'll have your mamma to answer to."

"Ugh." Faith finally releases her hold on my leg. "I can't stand some of the snooty folks in this town. I love planning the event, but attending it is an entirely different situation."

"Just bring your smile, Faith. They love you and will open their pocketbooks with your sweet talkin'. Think of all the children your few hours of misery will help." Mr. Ridley winks at Faith, but she barely cracks a smile. "Brooks, wear a suit tonight, please."

I rub my palms down the front of my jeans as panic starts to set in. "Um."

*Shit.* I don't have anything high class for an event like this. The closest thing I have is a vintage dress shirt I grabbed from the Goodwill the day I signed the contact for Ridley Racing. Somehow, I don't think it's swanky enough for a charity ball with the rich folk.

"Faith will take you to get one," he adds as he digs in his pocket. "She'll have you lookin' polished in no time."

"We may need the rest of the day off to get him in tip-top shape. Is that okay, Daddy?" She bats her eyelashes in his direction with such a sweet smile that she even gets me excited about the idea of shopping.

"Sure, baby. Whatever you need. Put it on the company card too. I don't want Brooks spending a dime from his own pocket."

"Can I get the afternoon off too?" Roscoe sweeps the napkin across his face, trying to hide his shit-eating grin.

"No, son. You have enough clothes. I need you in the garage with me this afternoon."

Roscoe's smile vanishes, and the grumbly guy from earlier

returns. “Fine. Shopping with Faith is hell on earth anyway.”

“I’ll get you a new tie, Roscoe.” She smiles at him before finally turning toward me. “Ready? We have a lot of work to do.”

“Um,” I mumble.

“Enjoy,” Roscoe says as Faith stands at the edge of the booth, waiting for me to follow.

I blow out a quick breath, not sure if I’m ready to learn what he meant by hell on earth, but I have a feeling I’m about to find out. How bad could it be, anyway? A few hours alone with Faith could never be a bad thing.

## FAITH

Shopping with Brooks is an experience I would rather not repeat. The man hates anything that’s not made of cotton or denim. We’ve spent over two hours picking out suits, dress shirts, and ties for him to try on, and he’s bitched and moaned the entire time. He keeps looking at the price tags and sneaking the clothes back on the racks when I am not looking. He seriously needs an overhaul if he is going to hang out with the Ridleys. Dad doesn’t do anything small, especially parties. This is an event the entire town will be talking about for months, and I can’t risk Brooks walking in looking like some small-town farm boy who just climbed down from a tractor. He can pull it off. The man could wear a garbage bag and still look damn hot, but my dad wouldn’t be happy in the least.

“Let me see.” I pace outside the dressing room, almost wearing a path into the carpet and trying not to lose my cool.

“I look like an idiot, Faith.” A hanger drops to the floor,

and Brooks curses.

"Get your ass out here and let me be the judge of that." My profanity earns me a stern look from a nosy saleswoman. I smile and wave, mouthing an apology when all I really want to tell her is to get lost. "I'm sure you look fine."

He fills out a ratty shirt and jeans like he stepped right out of a swanky country cologne commercial. Why would a suit be any different?

"If by fine you mean a complete nerd, then yeah, I pull it off."

I roll my eyes and drop my head forward. The man is impossible. He's full of cockiness and swagger, but throw a stylish suit on him, and he becomes self-conscious. Suddenly the door creaks open, and I hold my breath, waiting for Brooks to emerge.

First, a bare foot, then a leg covered in black fabric, and then the entire suit-covered man steps out of the dressing room. He's bathed in the overhead lighting, looking like he stepped out of my wet dream. My mouth waters, and I clutch my chest. I'm speechless.

He stares at me with his hands tucked into his pockets and waits.

I gawk. It is all I can do. The suit is pure perfection on him. It hugs the lines of his body in all the right places and makes him look like he just stepped out of a rugged *GQ* photoshoot about a billionaire businessman who likes to rough it on the weekends.

"Well?" he says with wide eyes. "I told you I look stupid."

"Wait." I finally find my voice as he starts to walk back

toward the doorway. I twirl my fingers in the air with a small smile. "Turn around."

I don't need him to turn around, but the greedy side of me, the one who's completely attracted to him, wants to see the entire package from every angle. The suit doesn't wear him in the least bit. If I ran into him on the street in the outfit, I'd swear it was custom made for his body. The black fabric is perfect, and the red tie with the crisp white shirt even makes the scruff on his face work.

He sighs loudly and pulls his hands from his pockets before turning in a tight circle. "This doesn't work."

"It looks good on you, Brooks."

He glances down with his eyebrows drawn together like he doesn't believe a word I'm saying. "Yeah?"

I nod quickly and take a step forward to make a few adjustments near his shoulders. "You wear it well."

"I feel like my high school principal."

I highly doubt his high school principal from the middle of nowhere Tennessee wore a three-thousand-dollar suit a day in his life. I smooth out the jacket and pull the cuff of his dress shirt out a little near his hands. "You look like a million bucks."

"I don't like the red tie."

I step back and take in the entire package, waving my hand and dismissing his comment. "Is there anything you do like?"

"The way the fabric caresses my dick." He touches himself and closes his eyes. "It's quite nice."

"You went commando?" I raise my eyebrows, shocked he didn't bother to mention that fact before he disappeared inside the dressing room. Laughter bubbles out of me, and the saleswoman pops her head around the corner, probably about to call security.

"Uh, yeah. I never wear underwear." He grabs his crotch and moans softly. "It's like the softest hands holding me. Kind of like yours, Faith."

Right on cue, the saleswoman steps into the dressing room and clears her throat. "Do you need any help in here?"

"No, ma'am. We're going to be purchasing a few suits." I dig in my purse and grab the company credit card. "Why don't you hold my charge and give us some privacy. We'll be done in a little while."

She snatches the card from my fingers and smiles. "A few suits?"

"Yes, ma'am. We need an entire wardrobe."

She smiles, almost laughing, and her entire demeanor changes. I'm sure she's already started to salivate after calculating the amount of commission she is about to make on our very large purchase.

She shuffles backward and dips her head. "Take all the time you need. I'll close this dressing room off and give you privacy. If you need anything, just holler. My name is Eileen."

"Thanks, Eileen." Then it dawns on me. Maybe Brooks needed to hear someone else's opinion before he'd finally believe he looked damn fine in that suit. "How do you think he looks in the suit? Should we buy it?"

Her eyes sweep up Brook's body before she nods her approval. "He's a stunner," she says before she leaves the room and closes the door behind her.

"See?" I cross my arms and know that Daddy will be

proud of how well he cleaned up.

"She's paid to say I look good. I could probably wear a thousand-dollar hot-pink tutu, and she'd say the same damn thing."

I laugh as I picture him making pirouettes in lace and a leotard. "*That* I'd love to see."

Brooks finally moves in front of the three-way mirror and takes a good look at himself. He makes a few faces and turns slightly to the left and then to the right, checking himself out. "Maybe I don't look like a total asshat."

I walk up behind him and stare at his reflection in the mirror. "You're kind of hot in that suit."

His eyes meet mine, and a small smile tugs at his lips. "How hot?"

"You might get lucky." I wiggle my eyebrows playfully.

He turns and wraps an arm around my back, pulling me against him. "Why, Ms. Ridley, I may walk around in this getup every damn day if it turns you on."

I admit that just about everything he wears turns me on. I almost hate myself for wanting him. He's everything I have tried to avoid my entire life but the only thing I seem to crave.

He leans forward. "Are you daydreaming about me again, princess?"

"No," I whisper against his lips.

He smirks. "We have the room to ourselves."

"We can't." I push against his chest.

I know what's going to happen next, and it could quite possibly land us both in jail. I can picture my god-awful mugshot on the evening news, and it's not a pretty sight.

"We can," he says and walks me backward. "Live a little."

His arm is around my waist, and before I can say another word, he covers my mouth with his lips, sweeping his tongue inside and tangling around mine.

I hate myself in this moment, but that does not stop me from letting Brooks pull me into the tiny dressing room with him.

I open my eyes and pull my mouth away from his. "What if she comes in?"

"She won't." He hikes up my skirt, stopping near my waist, and slides his hands to my bare ass. "Fuck," he moans, grinding his hard cock against me.

I'm about to protest as the cool air hits my ass, but Brooks drops to his knees, and suddenly I have nothing to say. The oxygen in my lungs evaporates, and the words I'm about to mumble disappear. I want him. I want to feel his wet mouth against my skin, devouring every bit of my need. I flatten my hands against the wall and brace myself for what's about to come next.

His lips scorch my flesh as he moves his face between my legs and sweeps his tongue through my wetness. My knees go weak, shaking from need, and I'm about to collapse. His arms wrap around my thighs, and I glance down as Brooks lifts my legs over his shoulders. I tangle my fingers through his hair and hold his face against me, more turned on than I've ever been.

*Damn.* He's so good at this. When his tongue swipes across my clit, my back arches off the wall, and I gasp for air. I want to cry out, beg for him to give me the orgasm that's quickly building, but I can't. We're in public, no matter how hard I try to forget. He pushes his fingers inside me, filling me completely.

I bite my bottom lip to stop myself from crying out as my back scrapes against the wall. My eyes are fixed on the mirror behind his back as he ravages my flesh, transfixed and completely lost in the moment. “Brooks,” I moan quietly, but I don’t know if I’m begging him for more or pleading with him to stop.

He growls against my core and closes his mouth around me, sucking my tender flesh as his fingers plunge deeper. I stop fighting and give in, letting the pleasure radiate through my entire body. Unable to stop, too turned on and close to the edge, I close my eyes and let go. My muscles tense and my toes curl as I dig my heels into his back, pushing his face harder against me. The mind-numbing orgasm crashes over me. Wave after wave of pleasure grips my body as I cry out, unable to stop the ecstasy from spilling from my lips.

Brooks doesn’t stop. His tongue toys with my clit, drawing out the orgasm as my body shudders in his arms. As soon as his fingers leave me, I miss the fullness. I’m dizzy as he lowers my feet to the floor. I push the hair that had fallen free away from my face and lean back against the wall, needing support with the way my knees are wobbling. Brooks Carter has a way of scrambling my brain like no one’s ever done before.

His fingers dig into my hip as he pulls me away from the wall. “Place your palms on the bench,” he says.

My eyes lock on his, knowing he’s not done with me yet. His eyes blaze, burning with lust as he watches me, waiting for me to move. My body shudders with delight as he guides my movement. As my hands flatten against the bench and I bend at the waist, I hear the familiar ticking of his zipper and glance over my shoulder as he pulls out his cock and palms the length in his hands. I lick my lips with eyes locked on his cock, more turned on by watching him touch himself than I would've expected.

"Eyes forward, princess." His front rests against my back as he sweeps the head of cock across my waiting flesh, and I stare down at the bench. "So fucking wet." he says, slowly pushing inside me.

I swallow hard and squeeze my eyes shut, unable to say anything back when his length is buried deep inside me. His warm breath skids across my ear, sending shivers down my spine as he pulls his cock out quickly and thrusts forward even faster. My body jolts forward, and I'm rocked onto my tiptoes from the powerful movement and his weight. His fingers bite into my skin near my hip, tightening as he plunges into me and impales me on his cock.

"Touch yourself."

I freeze. No one's ever said those words to me.

"Come for me."

Slowly, I slide my fingers between my legs and press against my clit. Sparks of pleasure shoot through my body as my pussy constricts around his hardness.

"So fucking sexy," he moans.

I ride my fingers with my eyes closed, bouncing off his cock as he pummels me from behind. His smooth motion becomes erratic as a second wave of pleasure, stronger than the first, sweeps through my body, rendering me motionless and unable to breathe. I gasp as his teeth sink into my shoulder, sending a new jolt of electricity throughout my already-spent body. He grunts, grinding into me and spilling his seed inside my body once again.

"We can't do this again," I say, suddenly riddled with guilt about everything. I pull my skirt down and try to control my labored breathing as panic starts to set in at the severity of the entire situation.

By situation, I mean my uncontrollable lust for Brooks.

"I'm sorry," he says, pushing the dress pants down his leg with his cock still wet from the most erotic sexual experience of my life. "I'll get a box of condoms. You shouldn't be too worried."

I narrow my gaze. "Why shouldn't I be worried?"

"I'm clean. I can't have kids, so there's nothing to worry about there. Plus, even if I could, you're on the pill."

My head jerks back, and I'm shocked by his admission. *He can't have kids?* I can't even imagine dealing with something as big as that. "What? Why would you think that?" I suddenly feel like the world's biggest asshole.

"Football accident back in high school. Doctor said it would be a miracle if I could ever have any." He shrugs it off like it's no big deal, but it has to be.

I press my palm against his chest, feeling the steady beat of his heart through his shirt. "I'm so sorry, Brooks."

"It's no big deal. I'd just mess my kids up like my mother did me anyway." There's sadness in his blue eyes, even if he tries to pretend like never being a father doesn't bother him.

"Don't say that." I shake my head and lean into him.

"It's true. I'm better off never having my own, Faith. Some of us aren't meant for that type of responsibility." He presses his palm to my cheek, gently cupping my face. "Don't feel bad, princess. I don't."

I gaze up at him, seeing a swirl of emotion in his eyes. "Why didn't you tell me before?"

"It's not something I like to talk about. It's really no big deal."

I push myself up on my tiptoes, planting a soft kiss on his lips. "I'm sorry," I say after I back away, staring up at him with a broken heart. The ache I feel isn't because I want his babies. I just can't imagine this beautiful man not having little ones running around his house vying for his attention someday.

He smiles as the emotion I'd seen a moment ago disappears. "Anyway, my balls are my business. Unless they're in your mouth—then they're yours." He laughs and tries to make light of the situation, but it doesn't work. Not on me. "So, are we done here?" He drops his hand away from my face and kicks the expensive pants into the air, catching them in his hand.

"We'll take this suit and grab a few other items, but yes, you can get dressed."

I look at myself in the mirror in shock. There's no denying or hiding what exactly happened in here from the saleswoman. There is absolutely nothing I can do to salvage the mess he made of my hair or hide my swollen lips. There's only one thing I can do. I plan to walk out of the dressing room and ring up a bill of sale so obscene, the saleswoman won't even bat an eyelash at my freshly fucked look.

# CHAPTER SIX

## BROOKS

I tug at the tie around my neck as I stand in the foyer of the two-story Ridley Mansion, feeling completely out of my element. Faith lied to me. The way she described her childhood home, I pictured something a little more modest and less... giant. A small army could live here and still have plenty of room without bumping into each other.

My eyes sweep up the grand staircase lined with a wall of windows and covered in wide plank mahogany boards. A rustic chandelier hangs in the middle of the enormous space, with animal horns, maybe elk, intertwined with wrought iron.

I cannot imagine growing up in a place like this. Playing hide and seek would have been so much fun compared to my house, where my options were the clothes hamper, under a bed, or in the dryer. The game never lasted very long because my mother would forget to find me, but I suppose that was all part of her master plan after all.

"Brooks," Mr. Ridley says, entering the foyer as I stare upward and wonder if I belted out a tune, if there'd be an echo. "Look at you, my boy. Faith did you well."

"Yes, she did, sir." Somehow, I keep a straight face as I

shake his hand. He has no idea about the double meaning. I'd like to keep my dick attached and my career intact. Plus, I like living.

"Beau, introduce me to our new guest," a woman says and drapes herself over his shoulder.

I see the resemblance instantly. The way she smiles, the color of her hair, and her deep-green eyes are every bit a part of the girl I've been crushing on.

He glances over his shoulder at her. "Sweetheart, this is Brooks Carter. The boy I've been telling you about."

She dips her head and gives me a kind smile. "Brooks Carter, it's wonderful to finally meet you. I'm Mimi Ridley."

"Ma'am." I tip my head before capturing her hand in mine, kissing her skin and being a total gentleman. "This is a beautiful place you have."

They glance around the room, maybe seeing it through my eyes, or maybe they never take the time to appreciate the grandeur of the space. "It is. Isn't it?"

"Someday I want a place just like this." I can't imagine what it would be like to come home to this much room. Between my upbringing and living on the road so long, I have grown accustomed to small spaces with very little personal things, but I could quickly get used to something as big as this.

"If you're half as good as my husband says, Mr. Carter, you'll have a home like this soon enough. Now if you'll excuse me, I have to check on the champagne."

"I have a house full of people who are excited to meet you." Mr. Ridley hangs his arm around my shoulders and guides me toward the back of the house as his wife saunters away with the same sway to her hips that Faith has.

The collar of my shirt feels like a noose, and I tug on it, looking for a little reprieve. On the track, I can handle a hundred strangers watching me, but put me in a swanky room like this, and I find myself rendered stupid. "Is Faith here?" I sweep my eyes across the crowd, searching for her like she's my lifeline.

"Not yet." His hand tightens on my shoulder. "She's always fashionably late to these events."

A woman approaches in a red dress with a slit so high that if she moved the right way, I'd be able to see everything she *wasn't* trying so hard to hide. "Why, Mr. Ridley, who do we have here?" She extends her hand, eyes totally on me, even though she asked Mr. Ridley the question.

"This is Brooks, Ms. Constance. He's the newest member of my team." Mr. Ridley elbows me and gives me the side eye when I don't immediately take her hand. "Brooks, this is Ms. Constance. Her family has lived here since the town's founding."

I'm so out of my element. First, I usually know how to greet a woman, but only the types that hang out in bars or around the garage. Ms. Constance is in a league of her own, oozing wealth and attitude.

I take her hand, lean forward, and plant a quick kiss atop her skin. "It's entirely my pleasure, ma'am." I gaze up as she touches her chin to her shoulder, trying to pull off the innocent act, but there's nothing about this woman even remotely angelic.

I straighten and try to pull my hand away, but she tightens

her grip. "So, you're a race car driver?"

"I am." I nod as Mr. Ridley turns his back for a moment. I am hoping for a rescue, but it doesn't seem like one is coming as something else has his full attention. I've heard about women like Ms. Constance, throwing around their wealth and expecting to get everything they want without any pushback.

Ms. Constance takes a step forward and invades my personal space, but I don't dare back up. "I'd love to go for a ride sometime." She smirks as she places her hand on my chest. "I meant in your car, of course."

Mr. Ridley coughs and grabs Ms. Constance by the arm, maneuvering her away from me. "Ms. Constance, there's someone I'd love for you to meet," he says, saving me from a pile of shit because I didn't know how long I could stand there and remain a gentleman.

She glances over her shoulder at me as Mr. Ridley brings her across the room. By the way she's undressing me with her eyes, I have a feeling it's not the last time I'll see Ms. Constance tonight.

Roscoe strides across the room with his hand tucked into his pocket, looking every bit the rich kid with his sandy-brown hair plastered back with hair gel like a member of the original Rat Pack.

"Brooks." He lifts his chin, not bothering with anything more.

I dip my head. "Roscoe."

He motions toward Ms. Constance. "Don't let her age fool you. She's a wildcat in the sack."

I tilt my head and study him. "Really, man?" I never

imagined Roscoe as the type to fall for older women. Ms. Constance is beautiful, even though she's easily more than twenty years my senior, but I don't think I could ever sleep with her. Not because of her age but because of her entitled attitude and bold sexual prowess.

"Dude," he says, drawing out the word like a surfer kid. "You're telling me you wouldn't tap the fuck out of that?" From my side, he points in her direction as she bends over and gives the entire room a view of what she offers.

I shake my head and tear my gaze away from her ass before she catches me and gets the totally wrong idea. "She's not really my type, Ridley."

He slaps me on the back, knocking me forward. "Yeah. She's too refined for a guy like you."

"I prefer someone a little less high maintenance." I slide my hand into my pocket and mimic Roscoe's more elegant stance.

He nudges my ribs with his bony elbow. "You're missing out, buddy. There's nothing finer than a woman who knows what she's doing."

I bite my tongue and stop myself from saying something I know I shouldn't. If I didn't like Faith so much, I'd love nothing more than to throw sleeping with her in his face. But I can't do that. I know if I do, I'll not only crush her but kill any future I have with Ridley Racing and ruin any chance I have of being with Faith ever again. Whatever we have going is good. Something I'm not willing to spoil just because Roscoe's a complete asshole.

"Boys," Mr. Ridley says and saves me from listening to any

more of Roscoe's bullshit. "We added a new auction item this year."

I grab a glass of champagne off a waiter's tray as he passes by. I gulp it down as Mr. Ridley continues to talk, and my gaze wanders around the room. Every man in the place has on a tuxedo or a three-piece suit, and the women are wearing floor-length ball gowns in every shade of the rainbow.

Mr. Ridley scans the crowd and puffs out his chest, clearly in his element. "We're really excited to see how it goes over this year."

"What is it?" Roscoe sips his champagne, sticking his pinky finger out like something from a movie.

Mr. Ridley faces us, his eyes moving between Roscoe and me with a wicked little gleam. "Faith came up with the idea a month ago when she was worried we weren't going to raise enough money." He pauses as I wipe my mouth with the back of my hand. "We're auctioning off a date with you boys."

"What?" Roscoe's just as shocked at the news as I am. I have a mouthful of champagne and am just about to swallow when Roscoe opens and says, "I don't go out with just anyone."

I choke on the champagne as it slides down my throat, bubbles exploding in places nothing should be. I pound on my chest, happy that I can't speak, because I'd love to remind him of his earlier statement about Ms. Constance. Clearly, he doesn't have standards.

*A date?* What the hell am I going to do with a rich chick for an entire evening? I'm sure they're not into honky-tonks and cheap beer.

"You only have to spend a few hours with her. It's not

that big of a deal, and it should bring in a pretty penny too. You wouldn't want to let down the Children's Hospital, would you?" Mr. Ridley stares at Roscoe, using his dad guilt skills.

"No," Roscoe grumbles against the rim of his champagne glass and narrows his eyes.

Mr. Ridley smiles. "It's settled. You two are the first items up for bid. Who wants to go first?"

"I'll go first and get it over with. I'm sure we'll set the bar pretty high with me." Roscoe grins and glances at me out of the corner of his eyes. "Who doesn't want to spend a night with a champion?"

I resist rolling my eyes at his cockiness. Any woman in this place could spend an evening with Roscoe without spending a dime. His earlier statement about Constance proves that point.

"That's fine with me."

Mr. Ridley dips his head, acknowledging my statement. "I'll move the crowd onto the back terrace and get everything rolling."

"We'll be ready," Roscoe tells his father before he walks away.

"I hope Constance buys me," Roscoe says as he sets his nearly empty champagne flute on the small table next to us. "The woman sucks a mean dick."

"I don't think that's what your father had in mind when he said *date*."

He looks at me like I have three heads. "You're a killjoy, Brooks."

As I follow Roscoe through the crowd, I search for any

sign of Faith. I can't imagine she'd be *this* fashionably late for a party she probably spent months planning. My heart leaps when I think I see her, but when the woman turns, it's Mrs. Ridley, and I feel more alone than I did before.

## FAITH

"God damn piece of shit. Of all nights." I kick the tire to my broken-down pickup truck with the tip of my high heel and let out a strangled cry. "You had to do this now!"

Something howls in the darkness and sends a shiver down my spine. I slap my hand over my mouth and freeze, praying it's just a dog and not a famished coyote looking for an easy mark. I'm less than a mile away from my parents' house, broken down on a dirt road, and no rescue in sight.

I turn my face toward the star-filled sky and shake my head. Not only did I forget my cell phone at home, but there's not a person attending the party who would be caught dead on this pot-hole-riddled dirt road. I laugh into the nothingness and give myself exactly thirty seconds to lose my shit.

When the hilarity of the situation wears off, I grab my purse from the front seat and my keys from the ignition and head toward my parents' house. My feet ache with every step, and curse words spill from my lips like one of the mechanics in our garage. What should've been a ten-minute walk feels like it takes forever. Walking in heels has never been an issue for me, but tonight, under the glow of faint moonlight, I'm getting a full workout. The rocks crunch under my feet, almost throwing me off balance. Just when I'm about to give up, the faint familiar glow rises from the dark horizon. I have never been so happy to see my childhood home as I am right now.

I burst through the front door, sweaty and with my thousand-dollar red-soled shoes covered in dirt. I'm greeted by one of the waitstaff, and based on the look on his face, I know I look like a total mess.

I smile and wave my hand wildly through the air. "Car trouble," I try to explain, but he wanders away without saying a word.

I catch a glimpse of myself in the mirror near the base of the stairs. I look better than I would've imagined. My hair is barely out of place, and besides a fresh sheen of sweat, I look exactly like I did when I ran out of my loft in a tizzy.

The house is empty besides the few waiters carrying trays toward the back of the house. I glance at the clock and stow my purse and keys in the coat closet. "Damn," I groan when I realize I missed the start of the auction.

My father's voice booms loudly as he announces the first item. I resist the urge to kick off my shoes even though my pinky toes feel like they're on fire. When I make my way to the back, my father is perched on the upper terrace with Roscoe and Brooks behind him.

My stomach rolls as I realize what's about to happen. When I came up with the genius idea to auction off the boys, I never imagined I'd have a thing for the new guy. *It's for charity.* I remind myself of that fact over and over again as I lean against the wall and take in the scene before me.

"Let's start with Roscoe Ridley. Ladies, if you'd like to go on a date with the reigning champ, now's your chance. Remember, one hundred percent of the proceeds will benefit the local Children's Hospital. We're starting the bidding at five hundred dollars. Do I have an offer?" My father waves his hand over the crowd, waiting for the first bid to roll in.

We both figured Roscoe would be the biggest prize of the night. The event may be for charity, but there isn't a person in attendance who doesn't want to *win* an item. They never liked to be outdone in any situation, especially when they're flashing their money in front of others.

Ms. Constance, the town trollop, is the first to raise her hand. "I'll take him off your hands for five hundred, Beau." She looks around, a giant smile on her blood-red-stained lips.

My father dips his head acknowledging her bid. Roscoe takes a few steps forward and opens his suit jacket before spinning in a circle to show what he has to offer. The man really thinks he's the hottest thing on the planet, and based on the typical fan reaction, he's right.

I drag my eyes to Brooks and let my mind wander. I picture him laughing, holding hands, and flirting with one of the rich ladies at the party. My pulse quickens, and I squeeze my hands together into tight fists. "Shit," I whisper, hating the reaction I'm having at the thought of someone else touching him.

"One thousand," a lady in the back yells and outbids Constance.

"We have one thousand. Do I have fifteen hundred?" My father turns to Roscoe and winks.

Constance glances over her shoulder at the woman in the back, probably throwing all kinds of hate with her eyes. "Fifteen hundred!"

“Two thousand.” Mrs. Peabody, the town’s newest divorcee, gives Constance a smug smile.

Their fight isn’t just about Roscoe—it’s personal. “Three thousand!” Constance raises her hand high in the air and waves her fingers.

“Five,” Mrs. Peabody replies.

Constance’s face turns red. “Seven,” she shouts.

My mouth falls open at the amount of money they’re throwing around. I’m not going to complain, because every penny is for a good cause, but damn. Their bidding war is no longer about my brother and has everything to do with the fact that Constance slept with Mrs. Peabody’s husband while they were very much man and wife, and the entire town knew about the affair.

My father is dumbfounded as he tries to keep up with the bidding war.

“Ten!”

I almost stumble backward with the insanity of the entire situation. Ten thousand dollars for a date with Roscoe is beyond ridiculous, even for these two ladies, who don’t value a dollar.

Constance takes a step forward, parting the crowd with her hands before giving Mrs. Peabody a nasty glare. “Fifteen. I can keep going as long as you can, Peabody.”

Brooks nervously yanks on his tie and shifts his weight between his feet. I feel a little guilty I didn’t warn him about the auction, but I’m sure he didn’t balk at the idea when he saw how happy the entire thing made my father.

Mrs. Peabody crosses her arms and ignores Constance. “Twenty.”

The crowd gasps before their heads snap, almost in unison, toward Peabody, waiting for her response. The board at the Children's Hospital is going to be beyond ecstatic for this year's donation. Between Roscoe and Brooks, we'll make more than double our usual donation.

Constance spins on her heels to face Mrs. Peabody, places her hands on her hips, and grins. "You can have him. I'll take the new boy."

Bile rises in my throat at the thought of Constance spending any time with Brooks. She's as handsy as they come and has absolutely no morals. Knowing Constance, she'll be on her knees begging to suck his cock before the entrée is even served. I cover my mouth and swallow the bitterness.

"I plan to have them both," Mrs. Peabody responds.

Roscoe leans over and whispers in Brooks's ear. A moment later, they both laugh like they've been best friends for a lifetime.

"Twenty thousand going once." My dad pauses as his eyes sweep across the crowd. "Twenty thousand going twice."

Roscoe blows on his nails and rubs them against his jacket, putting his cockiness on full display. It's nothing new to these people. They've watched Roscoe grow up and know exactly the kind of man he is. For all his flaws, he has a good heart and would do anything for his family.

"The date is sold to Mrs. Peabody," my dad announces, "for twenty thousand dollars."

Roscoe raises his hands in triumph, and the people in the crowd murmur.

"You're up, buddy." Roscoe slaps Brooks on the back

before pushing him toward my father and straight into the lion's den. "Good luck."

Brooks laughs nervously, looking more like a timid school boy than a champion race car driver in the making. My body stiffens as I watch the women undress Brooks with their hungry eyes. I want to shout *he's mine*, but I can't, and it eats me up inside.

Roscoe turns, finally catching sight of me, and smiles as he struts my way. He's impressed with himself, but I knew he'd fetch a pretty penny, especially from his rich old lady fan base. "Hey, you made it. What the hell happened?" he asks as he slides next to me.

"My truck broke down."

"You should've called. Why don't you just use the company car already?" Roscoe asks.

"I love my truck. When it won't run anymore, I'll buy my own car."

"You always have to be so hardheaded." Roscoe bumps his shoulder against mine. "We were worried about you."

"Looks like you were out of your mind with grief." I wave my hand in his face and try to silence him.

My dad wraps his arm around Brooks's shoulder and brings him closer to the railing so the crowd below can get a better look. "Ladies and gentlemen, this is Brooks Carter, the newest addition to Ridley Racing." The crowd cheers and claps while my father pauses for dramatic effect. "He's ruled the dirt, and now he's ready to play with the big dogs. Which one of you lovely ladies would like to spend an evening with Brooks, the newest sensation to hit the professional circuit?"

"Me!" Constance lurches forward like she is about to climb the staircase and hurl herself into Brooks's arms. "Give him to me."

"Now, Ms. Constance," Dad chides but softens his tone with a kind smile. "You know how this works."

"Two thousand," Constance calls out before my dad has even stated the opening bid.

Dad laughs and tips his head to her. "I have two thousand for Brooks. Do we have twenty-five hundred?"

"Five thousand," Mrs. Peabody replies, stepping through the crowd to stand nearly shoulder to shoulder with Ms. Constance.

*Oh Lord.* This could get even nastier in a hot minute.

"It looks like we have another bidding war," I say to Roscoe.

He crosses his arms over his chest and throws his shoulder back. "He won't go for more than me."

I laugh softly. "We'll see."

"Ten," Constance replies.

"Fifteen!"

"Twenty!"

Within seconds, they meet the bid they set for Roscoe and are chomping at the bit to go even higher. Brooks stands there, silent and frozen as he stares down at the two women.

"Well, fuck," Roscoe hisses at my side. His overinflated ego smashes to smithereens right before my eyes.

I bite my bottom lip to stop myself from calling out a higher bid. I don't want either of these women to spend a single second alone with Brooks. Even though he's not mine, the knot in my stomach doesn't seem to know the difference.

I'm so consumed by the noise in my head, I don't hear the final bid before my dad announces, "Sold for thirty-five thousand dollars."

"Fuck," I groan as I snap my gaze to two women who were just fighting over Brooks. By the smile on Constance's face, I'd say she is the victor. I cover my face and let a string of words that would have gotten my ass tanned as a child burst free.

"You okay?" Roscoe touches my arm.

"I'm just so excited," I say, plastering a fake smile on my face.

Constance is running up the stairway and heading straight for Brooks. He backs up, looking stiff but bracing himself for what's coming. She leaps into his arms, and he spins around, holding her like a bride. He's playing the part perfectly, but when his blue eyes meet mine, they narrow to slits.

Brooks Carter is pissed, and there's going to be hell to pay.

# CHAPTER SEVEN

## BROOKS

Faith disappears into the house before I can untangle Constance from my body.

"Don't run off so fast." The woman latches her arms tighter around my neck every time I try to wiggle free.

"Constance, I'm sure Mrs. Ridley would like to get your check before we actually start our date. Don't you think, doll?"

She blushes and blinks her eyelashes rapidly as she stares up at me. "I love when you call me that."

I resist the overwhelming urge to drop her flat on her ass. "We have time for this," I say, playing into her fantasy but hating every minute of it.

"You're right. I need to give my donation so we can get to the good stuff." She slides down my body and places her hands on my chest. "I just know you're going to be worth every penny." She slowly peels her hands away from me, and she walks away, swaying her hips for effect. She glances at me over her shoulder, as if to make sure I'm enjoying her show.

I stand there, waving to her and wishing she'd move her ass a little faster so I can find Faith. When Constance is finally out of sight, I wait ten seconds before I take off through the house, searching each room I pass for any sign of Faith. By the time I make it into the foyer, I spot her halfway up the stairs.

I take the steps two at a time and grab her arm before she makes it to the first landing. "Where the hell were you?"

"I broke down."

Moving closer, I pin her back against the wall and invade her personal space. "Why didn't you call? I've been worried sick."

She finds her bearings and pushes off the wall, squaring her shoulders and pushing against my chest. "I forgot my phone. What business is it of yours, anyway?"

I grip her arm again and bring my face close so only she can hear me. "Less than ten hours ago I had my dick buried so deep inside you I could feel you breathe. That's why it's my fucking business."

Her eyes flash with anger or maybe lust, but they change, burning brighter than I've seen before.

"Faith," Mrs. Ridley says from the bottom of the staircase, and I release Faith and back away. "Is everything okay up there?"

"Yes, Mamma." Faith narrows her gaze before stepping around me to peer over the banister. "Brooks was worried about me. We're just talking."

"Your father and I were wondering what happened to you, dear."

I can't turn around. I'm angry with myself for being so stupid and reckless. I knew we weren't in private, but I let my aggravation get the better of me.

"I'm here now. Sorry," Faith says and glances back at me,

giving me an *oh-fuck-we-almost-got-caught-you-asshole* face before turning back around. "Can you give us a few moments alone, Mamma?"

"Why don't you finish the conversation upstairs in private. I'd hate for someone to get the wrong idea."

I squeeze my eyes shut and tilt my head back, cursing under my breath. Here it is. Mrs. Ridley saw everything. My entire career is about to go up in flames because I let my emotions get the better of me.

"Thanks. We'll be quick." Faith grabs my arm and pulls me up the rest of the stairway. I still can't turn around or acknowledge Mrs. Ridley, even though I know I should, but I just can't.

I follow Faith through the first open door. "I'm sorry," I say as she slams the door.

"She won't say a word to Daddy." She rubs her fingers down her cheeks.

"I didn't mean for that to happen. I don't know what came over me."

"What's your issue, Brooks?"

I touch my chest, dipping my chin as I raise my eyebrows. "My issue?"

She places her hands on her hips and drops a shoulder. Her fiery side shows, and it's sexy as hell. "Yeah. Your. Issue."

"I was worried." I push my hands through my hair, and I know I'm going to sound like a complete asshole, but I say it anyway. "You didn't even call. No one knew where you were. Something really bad could've happened to you."

"I'm a grown-ass woman, Brooks Carter. I know how to

look after myself. Anyway, you're going to have a grand time with Ms. Constance."

I storm toward her, and all the emotions I felt earlier come roaring back double-fold. She backs up as I take two strides, closing the space between us.

"You jealous?" I lean forward, sliding my hands around her waist, and hover my lips less than an inch away from hers. "Tell me you don't care, princess."

She narrows her eyes as I slide my hands behind her back and cup her ass. Her breathing becomes labored, and I move my lips closer, keeping my eyes locked on her. She tangles her fingers in my hair and pulls my face closer. "Kiss me already," she whispers.

I gaze into her deep-green eyes and let out a strangled growl before I crash my lips down on hers. She moans into my mouth as she wraps her legs around my waist and tugs on my hair. In seconds, my dick is hard as a rock. My grip on her ass tightens as she grinds against my cock.

She pulls away and gasps for air. "I need to feel you inside me, Brooks."

I moan, capturing her lips with mine again, and start to carry her toward the bed and stop. "We shouldn't do this," I tell her, pained by the very words leaving my mouth before she pulls my mouth back to hers.

There's a knock on the door, and we both freeze. "Hello!"

My eyes fly open, and Faith's eyes widen. We freeze, barely breathing for fear of being caught.

"Is someone in there?" a woman asks as the handle starts to turn.

"One minute!" Faith calls out, pushing against my chest and sliding down my body. "Please use another room. This one is private and not for guests."

"Sorry about that. I was looking for the bathroom."

"Down the hall on the right, ma'am."

The handle releases and goes just as still as I am.

"Thank you!"

I collapse onto the bed, rolling onto my back and sporting a full hard-on. The moment's gone, but it's probably for the best. We are playing with fire messing around in her parents' house. The woman probably saved us from making a bigger mistake than we already had.

Faith stands at the foot of the bed and exhales. "That was too close. Maybe we should take a break for a little while."

We stare at each other for a moment before I decide it's time I man up and do the right thing. Or at least try to anyway.

"Yeah." I let out a huff and push myself upright. I'm not sure if I can keep my hands off Faith now that I've had a taste. Everything about her calls to me. I crave her, and working as close to her as I'm going to be over the next few months isn't going to make anything any easier.

We've known each other less than two days, and she's quickly become an addiction.

## FAITH

My mother's waiting for us at the bottom of the stairs as Brooks follows behind me. "Faith. Can I have a word?"

"Sure," I say with a smile, trying to pretend like she didn't just catch me red-handed.

But my mother doesn't return my smile as she peers over my shoulder. "Brooks, Mr. Ridley was asking for you. He's out back."

I stand completely still as I stare at my mother and try to figure out if she's pissed at me or not. Knowing her, she's going to have a lot to say, and some of it won't be pretty. That's the thing about her. She's honest and blunt but never cruel. She's never been one to hold her tongue, especially when it involves my brother or me.

"Thank you, Mrs. Ridley." I can hear the tension in his voice.

I glance in his direction as he walks away, and the pained smile on his face as his eyes meet mine tells me he knows we're in for a world of hurt. When I tear my gaze away from his, I find my mother staring straight at me without a smile or any hint of amusement.

"Do you know what you're doing?" She sets her champagne glass on one of the stairs and steps closer.

"I don't know what you mean." I play dumb because I'm not ready to admit a damn thing. Not yet at least.

"You were upstairs for far too long, and your hair..." She reaches out, brushing a few of the strands over my shoulder that fell free during our kiss. "You're playing with fire, Faith."

"Mamma." I squeeze my eyes shut, dropping my head forward, and know when to wave the white flag. "I'm sorry. I swear nothing happened up there."

She places her hand on my shoulder and squeezes. "Don't be sorry."

I lift my head, shocked by her words.

"But you know he works for us, and your brother is having a hard time with this. What would your father think if he knew about you two?" She raises an eyebrow.

"You can't tell them." I grab her arm and start to beg. "Please, Mamma. It won't happen again. We only kissed."

Technically I wasn't lying to her. Just now, we did only kiss. It would've led to a lot more if the lady hadn't interrupted us, though.

"He's only been here a few days, Faith. I'd hate for you to have your heart broken."

"I won't get hurt. We were just talking, and things got out of control for a second. Whatever happened is over. It was a momentary lapse in judgment and won't happen again."

"Do you like him?"

"Yes. I don't know how." I grit my teeth and clench my hands at my side, because admitting the truth for the first time is harder than I ever imagined. "We just met, but I like him too much."

"Don't string him along unless you're willing to love a man like that. From everything your daddy has told me about Brooks, they sound like two peas in a pod. Men like them love fierce and hard, just like they drive, baby. You're playing with fire if you make him fall in love with you and try and walk away. I tried it with your daddy, and I ended up pregnant."

My mouth falls open and I gawk at her. "I thought...wait."

My mind's reeling, and I do some quick calculations in my head. "I thought you were married and got pregnant on your honeymoon?"

She tips her head back and laughs. "We talked about

marriage, but I wasn't ready to fully commit to your father. He was a race car driver with big dreams, and I didn't want to hold him back. He wasn't stupid. He knew well enough that if he knocked me up, I'd have to marry him." She smiles so big. "Back then unwed mothers were not looked upon so kindly here in Buxton. I should've been mad, but I couldn't be. I could've never loved another man the way I loved your daddy."

"Wow," I say, too shocked to say anything else.

"All men are fragile creatures, even your daddy and especially young ones like Brooks."

"It's been forty-eight hours. We're not in love."

"Keep lyin' to yourself. I loved your father from the moment I laid eyes on him."

"I think you're wrong, Mamma. Brooks doesn't care about me."

"I saw the way he was looking at you as you came down the stairs."

I want to tell her we called everything off and decided it was best if we didn't put ourselves in any situation that may lead to us falling into bed together, but I couldn't.

"Daddy's coming."

"We'll talk about this later. For now, spend time with our guests and not so much time upstairs."

My dad joins us, wrapping his arms around my mother's middle and burying his face in her hair. "My two favorite girls in the world. People are asking where you ran off to."

She places her hand over his and tilts her head toward his. "Faith was just helping me with something, sweetheart."

"Are you done?" His eyes meet mine. "Faith, is everything

okay? You look a little disheveled?"

My mother answers before I have a chance to open my mouth. "Yes. Don't worry, Beau, everything's fine."

"Um," I mumble and run my hands down the sides of my dress. "My truck broke down on the back road, so I was later than I planned. I had to walk the rest of the way here."

"Well, shit, baby girl. Why did you not call me?"

"I forgot my phone. I'm sorry I missed the auction, Daddy."

"It's okay. We raised a ton of money thanks to your brilliant idea." He's practically beaming when he tells me the news.

I smile even though the entire thing has backfired in my face. "That's great, Daddy."

All I can think about is Ms. Constance and her greedy little fingers all over Brooks because of my lame idea. Every dime goes toward a great cause, but I'm not sure I can stomach knowing she'll do everything in her power to sleep with Brooks. I may not be able to have him again, but that doesn't mean I want someone else to have him either.

# CHAPTER EIGHT

### BROOKS

Ms. Constance sits across from me at Bella Donna, the best Italian restaurant in Buxton, wearing a sleek black cocktail dress with so many diamonds around her neck that no one's looking at her cleavage. She's sipping a glass of the most expensive champagne on the menu and, surprisingly, being a perfect lady. She barely even flirts with me. She insists we only have the best of everything, and I wasn't about to argue since she is picking up the tab.

"Do you ever get lonely?" She holds the champagne flute against her lips and stares at me over the rim. "You know, being on the road as much as you are?"

"Not really." At least I didn't think of myself as lonely. Sure, there were times when I wanted someone in my life to share my victories with at the end of a hard-fought weekend. But I'd never had that, not even as a kid, so I wasn't sure how not being by myself even felt.

That is...until Faith. We've successfully kept our distance after work hours, only interacting when completely necessary for the last few days. I leaned on the guys in the garage more, picking their brains and asking for their guidance when I needed help. It has been the slowest few days of my life.

Ms. Constance sets her drink on the table and touches the diamond necklace draped around her neck. "I do." She strokes the diamonds slowly and stares at the bubbles rising in her glass. "I was married once. Did you know that?"

I shake my head, settling back in my chair. "No, ma'am."

"I loved my husband." She giggles for a moment and covers her mouth with the back of her hand. "Husbands," she corrects herself. "Each one was very different. My first husband, Daniel, he was the best man I'd ever meet."

I toy with the napkin next to my plate but keep my eyes on her. "What happened? If you don't mind me asking."

She waves her hand and smiles softly. "No. I love talking about him, about us. We were only married a few years before he passed."

"I'm so sorry." For a moment, my heart aches for her. The loss she must've felt losing someone so soon after promising each other forever had to be unbearable.

"The hurt is still deep even after all these years."

I nod as I lean forward, resting my arms on the table. For all her flaws, sleeping with Mr. Peabody and her gossiping nature, I could see the woman dying to be loved underneath. "I'm sure it is."

"They say that eventually the sadness fades, but it's not true." She lifts her glass and takes a sip, staring into the distance.

"I can only imagine."

"I hope you never have to experience that kind of loss."

The Constance across the table is an entirely different

version of the woman I met at the charity auction. There's no innuendo or flirtation spilling from her lips. "I'm sorry I'm not acting like myself. This day is always hard for me. He's been gone thirty years, but it never gets any easier."

"We didn't have to go out tonight. We could've rescheduled."

She cracks a smile and shakes her head. "I needed to go out tonight more than ever. I wanted to sit across from a handsome man with my favorite necklace and just pretend for a little while. Does that make sense?"

"No. No. It makes perfect sense, Ms. Constance."

"I couldn't bear to sit at home alone tonight like I've done every year for the last three decades." She leans back in her chair as the waiter approaches with our dessert, but she waves him away. "Enough about me. Do you have a special lady in your life?"

"No one." I'm being truthful. Whatever small thing Faith and I had going is off, dead and buried. Not forgotten, though. I could never wipe the memories of how she felt, tasted, and smelled from my mind.

"A good-looking boy like you has to have women all over the country."

I laugh at how completely wrong she is, but I can see how she'd think that. Especially since she knows Roscoe as well as she does. I'm not a playboy. I don't bang anything with two legs just because I need sex. "I try to keep my life as uncomplicated as possible. My only focus right now is the long racing season ahead and nothing more."

"Smart kid." She pushes her empty champagne flute to

the middle of the table. "Sometimes it's better to not fall in love. Less heartbreak that way. It's better to bury yourself in something you can control."

"Yeah," I say with a sigh.

"The pro circuit is the real deal. You've made it to the big leagues, and I'm sure you'll have to beat the ladies off with a stick once they get a look at you."

I hadn't thought about the groupies and how things could quickly spiral out of control once the season started rolling. I was already seeing women camped out, dressed in Roscoe Ridley gear and following him around town like lost puppies. I wouldn't even know how to handle their nonstop flirtations, but Roscoe relishes that shit. He eats up every bit of it and takes what he wants without remorse. But I don't want just any girl. I only have eyes for Faith Ridley.

When we walk outside, Constance stops near the valet stand and hands the gentleman her ticket. "Thank you for a wonderful evening, Brooks, and for being a gentleman." She turns to me, and I brace myself for a kiss or at least an unwelcomed ass grab, but she does neither. She holds out her hand, much like she did when we met in the foyer for the first time.

I sweep her hand up to my lips and kiss her softly, maintaining eye contact the entire time. "Thanks for everything, Ms. Constance. Not just the donation to the Children's Hospital but for an enjoyable evening and good company too."

"Do me a favor, kid. Don't tell anyone about tonight or say nice things. I know I have a reputation in town, and I'd hate to ruin their image of me."

I laugh as I help her into her car.

## FAITH

I've been lying in bed, staring at the same spot on my ceiling for an hour. I can't stop thinking about Brooks's date with Ms. Constance. I'm torturing myself over a man I'm not even dating. I shake my head at the ridiculousness of the entire situation. With Marcus, I never thought about where he was or what he was doing, and he ended up right between the legs of my sorority sister.

I picture Constance touching Brooks, putting her hands on him—and more—so many times, he finally caves. I squeeze my eyes shut, force back the acid crawling up my throat, and try to wipe the disgusting image from my head.

I groan as soon as I start thinking about *them* again. Somehow, I've become *that* girl. The needy one sitting by her phone, waiting for a guy to call even though he won't. Why would he? I'm the one who called the whole thing off and made sure to put as much distance as possible between us. I promised myself I wouldn't dwell on what they could be doing, but no matter what I do, I can't get them off my mind.

I jump straight up when my phone buzzes at my side. I scramble to find the damn thing buried under a pile of blankets. "Shit," I hiss, throwing everything off the bed, and slide onto the floor when the phone *thumps* against the hardwood. I stare at the phone, reading each word from Brooks slowly.

*My obligation you so kindly put on my shoulders*

*without my knowledge or approval is complete.*

*Did she touch you?*

I hit send and immediately wish I could delete the message. *Oh, no.* I didn't mean to really ask him that. It's been on my mind all night, but I had no right to pry.

*You really wanna know?*

I gawk at the screen as my stomach turns. *Shit.* She touched him. He doesn't even need to answer because I know what kind of woman she is, and Brooks...well, he's a man.

*OMG. You kissed her!*

*No. Don't tell me.*
*It's none of my business.*

I smack my head against the side of the mattress over and over again as he types his reply. I'm expecting a long-winded response because he's taking forever, but all I get back is...

*Jealous?*

"Asshole!" I yell at the screen like he can somehow hear me. I rest my arms on my knees, drop my head forward, and take a deep breath. *He's not yours.*

I'm being irrational. We're nothing to each other. We shared a few kisses and had sex a couple times, but people do that and move on without a problem, right? I'm lying to myself, and I know it. I'm not the type of girl to have a physical relationship without my feelings getting involved. Brooks isn't any different. It may have been short-lived, but it was hot and consuming.

*Did you really kiss her?*

*Are you going to admit you're jealous?*

The man is impossible. But the problem is, he's right. I am a little jealous Constance was able to be seen in public with him while I sat at home alone. Even when Brooks and I were together, everything we did was in private. I'll never admit my jealousy, though, especially when it comes to Constance.

*I'm just concerned. I've known Constance my entire life.*

*She's really not that bad. She's actually a nice woman when you get to know her.*

My mouth falls open, and my fingers hover over the keys as I read his message again, figuring I hadn't read them right the first time. *She's not that bad?* I don't even know how that's possible with the shit she's pulled over the years. The woman is as rotten as they come.

*Now admit it... You're a little jealous.*

*Of Constance? Never.*

*Faith.*

*Brooks.*

*I thought about us tonight.*

The butterflies in my stomach flutter just like they did the first time I saw him.

*Me too.*

I'm smiling like an idiot, and then fear washes over me. What if he went out with Ms. Constance and realized he didn't want the complication that goes along with me? Maybe that's what he was thinking. He never said he was thinking good things about me, just that he thought about me.

*Want company? I could be in*
*your bed in under a minute.*

I rush to the window and peek through the blinds. Brook's truck is parked down the street in front of the bar that led to our first night together.

I type *Come here*.

And then erase it before sending my real message.

*Go home, Brooks.*

I walk away from the window and hesitate for a moment before pressing send. I want nothing more than to tell him to come up and spend the night. But too much is on the line, and we need his head in the race more than I need my Brooks fix. I hold my breath, switching my phone off because I can't bear to read his response. I crawl under the covers and bury my face until sleep pulls me under.

# CHAPTER NINE

## BROOKS

The place cleared out two hours ago, and no one else is around. I couldn't leave. My adrenaline is off the charts for the first time in years. I knew if I left, I'd never get a good night's sleep and would end up partying with the fans at the RV park or banging on Faith's door until she finally let me inside. I figured the best place for me was right here, alone, not doing anything to fuck up my future. I'm hunched over my car, checking under the hood, when Mr. Ridley walks into the garage.

"You ready for the race?" he asks, resting his arms on the frame and looking under the hood with me.

I've been gawking at the engine for hours. I haven't touched a thing because there wasn't anything that needed doing. The team made her purr after my practice run. She would be perfect for tomorrow's qualifying race. "Ready as I'll ever be, sir."

"I remember my first big-time race like it was yesterday."

"Yeah?"

"I want you to have fun tomorrow. Don't worry about winning. I don't expect that right out of the gate, but I want you to give it your best and enjoy the moment."

"I will. I promise." My heart's racing just thinking about tomorrow. I've dreamed about this moment for so many years, the fact that the day is already here is surreal. I'm itching to get on the track, bumping against the competition and proving I belong out there. The last thing I want is to make Mr. Ridley regret signing me to the team.

"Memorize the tiny moments. The sound of the car roaring at your side, the feel of the car as she rumbles underneath you, and the feeling of freedom as everything around you falls away except for the road in front of you."

I push myself off the car and straighten my back as I roll my neck to work out the kinks. I shouldn't have spent so long hunched over, but I couldn't stop looking at the car. *My car.* "I can't thank you enough for everything you've done for me."

"Listen, tonight Mrs. Ridley is having a family dinner. It's tradition. Normally it's just the four of us, but since you're one of us now, you are family too." Using two fingers, he strokes his beard and lowers his chin as he looks at me. "I've been told to relay the message that she's expecting your presence this evening."

"I'd be honored to come to dinner tonight," I say without any hesitation.

"Seven o'clock. Don't be late, or there will be hell to pay."

"I'm going to stick around here for a little bit longer. Then I'll shower and head over."

"Where are you staying anyway, Brooks?"

"Down by the tracks at Palm Court."

He draws his eyebrows down. "At the RV place?"

"Yeah, that's where I parked my rig." Rig makes the half-rusted hunk of metal sound fancy compared to the reality of what I own. The inside smells like dirt and sweat, but it is the closest thing to a home I've ever had.

"Why don't you bring a bag? You can stay the night with us."

I rub the back of my neck. The idea does sound nice, but I can't. "I wouldn't want to impose. I appreciate the offer, but I'm more than happy in my slice of heaven."

"I get it. There's no place like home." He starts to walk away but stops and turns. "And Brooks."

I lift my gaze, meeting his eyes. "Yeah?"

"I'm happy you're here, son," he says, his cheekbones rising as he gives me his signature toothy smile.

I rock backward, unable to speak for a minute. Mr. Ridley stands across the way, staring at me and waiting for some sort of reply, and somehow, I pull myself together long enough to say, "Thank you, Mr. Ridley."

He nods before closing the door.

"Damn," I mutter. He called me *son*.

I'm the luckiest bastard in the world. Who else can say they came from nowhere, without so much as a pot to piss in, and is handed a race car, sponsorship, and just about everything to make their dreams come true? No one except me. The small-town boy who came from the most humble beginnings imaginable finally has a chance to change his destiny and make something of himself.

For the first time in my life, I feel part of something bigger than myself. Mr. Ridley hasn't treated me like a punk kid he plucked from the streets but like a family member. I stare down at the ground and grin.

The man's been good to me. The Faith embargo that I've been under for the last week has to stay firmly in place. Not just for her sake but for Mr. Ridley's.

## FAITH

Roscoe's stretched out on the floor in his usual spot in front of the television. He's watching a recording of last season's final race. I've never known anyone so consumed with their own success as much as my brother. He's already watched the same race more than a dozen times, hollering at the screen when Jim Bo Fisher crashes into the wall, obliterating his car.

"Can we watch something else?" I groan, plopping down on the couch behind him. "Anything but this."

"What's better than this?" He doesn't bother turning around. "I mean, look."

I cross my arms over my chest and pout, wishing I could snatch the remote out of his hands.

My father's in the kitchen helping with the final dinner preparations. I stare at the clock, wondering where Brooks is, because he's about to be late. There's nothing worse in my mother's book than tardiness.

*Where are you?*

As soon as the message is delivered it immediately says *read.*

*In the driveway.*

I turn toward the front windows but only see darkness.

*It's almost 7.*

*I need a minute.*

*For what?*

There's a long pause, and I start to stand.

*I'm processing.*

I collapse back onto the couch. *Processing?* What the hell does that even mean? Men, especially Brooks, do the weirdest shit, and I don't think I'll ever understand what goes on in their heads.

*Are you losing it?*

*No, but this is kind of a big deal.*

*It's dinner. You're not meeting the president.*

*It's a family dinner. I've never had one, Faith.*

My fingers hover over the buttons, but I can't figure out

what to say. My heart hurts for Brooks and the shitty childhood he had. I spend so much time bitching about Roscoe that sometimes I know I sound ungrateful, but I can't imagine not being surrounded by the three people in this room.

*One minute. No pressure or anything.*

I try to make light of the situation, hoping he'll relax. I'm off the couch, heading toward the door, before he has a chance to knock.

"He's almost late," my mother says.

"He'll be on time, darling," Dad tells her as Brooks's feet touch the landing.

"He's here!" I yell out just as the grandfather clock in the foyer starts to chime.

I step backward, swinging the door open, and stare at him. "You okay?" I ask quickly.

He glances down and walks in without so much as a smile. "I'm fine," he says and doesn't make eye contact.

"But you..."

He finally looks me in the eyes, but there's no hint of the playful guy I started crushing on. "I'm okay, Faith, really."

My gaze drifts down his body. "You look nice tonight." He's wearing one of the new outfits I picked out, which makes me unbelievably happy. The man looks damn good in a cashmere sweater and blue jeans.

"Because of you." He smiles, but it doesn't reach his eyes.

"You wanna talk about what's bothering you?"

He stiffens. "No."

I reach for his hand, but he pulls away and my stomach drops. "Okay," I whisper.

"Boy," my dad yells from the kitchen, "get your ass in here!"

Brooks stares at me. He steps forward, and I think he's going to touch me. Not in a sexual way, but maybe he's going to touch my hand or brush his fingers against my face. I hold my breath, waiting for whatever is about to happen. The butterflies are back. They're doing acrobatics in my stomach, fluttering around like it's the first bit of sunshine after a rainy day. I lean forward, figuring I'd make it easier on him and letting him know I want the contact. Just when I think he's about to touch me, he moves to the side and walks away.

I spin around with my mouth hanging open as he enters the kitchen. Every bit of air whooshes out of me, and the butterflies crumple into a tight knot. I thought we were having a moment.

Things have been tense between us, but we've at least been cordial to one another. His actions aren't cruel, but I was expecting something...different.

"Thank you for coming, Brooks," Mamma says as I stand in the foyer, watching as he kisses her cheek.

"I'm honored to be here, ma'am. I brought you these as a thank-you." He hands her a bouquet of red roses.

"They're beautiful, Brooks." She touches his arm with one hand as she takes the flowers from him. "Mimi, please."

"Mimi." He smiles.

I stalk into the living room with my hands balled into tight fists and plop onto the couch. Roscoe glances backward and makes a face. I raise an eyebrow, challenging him to say something. He doesn't.

"Hey, asswad!" Roscoe yells from the floor, not bothering to get up because he can't tear his eyes away from his impending victory.

"Roscoe," Brooks replies.

"It's good you made it," Dad says, whipping potatoes into paste in the blender because he refuses to do them by hand.

"I wouldn't miss it," Brooks says loudly, trying to be heard over the electric mixer.

I cross my arms over my chest, narrowing my eyes on the back of Roscoe's head, and my mom places her hand on my shoulder. Maybe she senses my hostility. It's not like I'm hiding how I feel, even though I should.

"Bubba," Mamma says.

I laugh as Roscoe drops his head because he hates that nickname.

"It's time to eat, and we need some help getting everything to the table."

"I'll help, Mimi," Brooks says quickly.

When Roscoe doesn't move, Mamma releases her grip on my shoulder and moves toward him. "Bubba, I ain't gonna say it again."

As soon as he hears the click of her heels coming toward him, he pops up and marches toward the kitchen without making eye contact with her. He can act all tough and even be an asshole, but even the big, bad Roscoe is afraid of my mother. We all are. She's sweet as a peach, but when she's mad, she's liable to beat the tar out of anyone with the heel of her fancy shoe.

I push myself upward and follow Roscoe to the kitchen.

Mamma places the salad bowl in my hands. "What's wrong?" she leans in and whispers.

"Nothing. I'm great." I don't know why I bother to lie. She knows me better than anyone. To make matters worse, she knows that Brooks and I had a thing, but she doesn't know everything.

"Trouble with?" She jerks her head backward toward Brooks.

"There's nothing going on, Mamma. I'm just tired."

She clicks her tongue against the roof of her mouth. "I figured one of you would get hurt."

I grip the salad bowl tighter. "Not now, Mamma. Please," I tell her before marching toward the dining room.

Brooks is standing over the table holding the macaroni and cheese. "Wow," he says and shakes his head.

The table is completely decked out with the gold-trimmed white china, a linen tablecloth covered in twigs and pine cones, and more candles than I have fingers. "She doesn't do anything small," I tell him as I set the salad in front of my father's seat and take my usual place.

"Where do I sit?" he asks, but I don't answer.

"Sit next to me," Roscoe says as he slides the mashed potatoes and fried okra onto the table.

I roll my eyes. *When did they become best friends?*

My dad's staring into the bowl he's carrying when he walks in with my mother. "This is a little excessive."

She laughs. "I got a little carried away."

"I'd say so, but the coleslaw looks delicious, darling."

I resist the urge to roll my eyes again. Everyone's chipper and in a good mood except for me. Maybe Brooks too, but he's masking it well, putting on a good face in front of my parents. My dad sweeps my mom into his arms and plants a kiss on her lips. They look like something out of a movie. I expect her leg to sweep off the ground as he tightens his grip. My eyes drift to Brooks. He's watching them as they lock lips and put on a display, one that would earn me a stiff talking to about public displays of affection if the roles were reversed.

I want their kind of love. My father would move heaven and earth if it meant making my mother happy. I won't settle for anything less except the be-all kind of love they have even to this day.

As my parents sit down, Roscoe grabs the bowl of mashed potatoes.

"Put the bowl down, Roscoe. We haven't said grace yet," my mother tells him.

"I'm starving, though," he whines.

She gives him a pinched expression, and he quickly places the bowl back on the table.

"Hands," my dad says and nudges Roscoe.

My mother takes my hand in hers and glances across the table at Brooks. He gives me a blank stare as I slide the back of my hand across the table. I wiggle my fingers as a silent clue for him to give me his hand so my father can say a prayer. His gaze dips as his lips press together into a flat line before he slowly slides his warm callused palm against mine.

My father bows his head as I close my fingers around Brooks's hand. "Lord"—he pauses as the rest of us bow our heads—"we're thankful for the blessings you've bestowed upon us. We're blessed for a new season and family dinner. We're lucky to have a new face with us, dear Lord, and honored to have him sit amongst us. Please keep the boys safe on the track and watch over them during the season."

There's a long pause. Without lifting my head, I peer at Brooks, and he's staring at my father. I squeeze his fingers. He glances in my direction as I lift my head just an inch so he can see my eyes.

"And Lord..."

Brooks immediately shuts his eyes, dropping his face forward.

"Watch over my girls, the loves of my life. Keep them safe from harm because without them, we are nothing, and all of this is for naught. Amen."

"Amen," everyone says in unison.

My father, for all his manly eloquence and public speaking skills, doesn't do well with prayers. He tries. Lord, how he tries, but there's always something awkward about the entire thing.

Brooks releases my hand far too quickly and pulls his arm back to his side of the table. "Everything smells delicious, Mimi," he says with the brightest smile.

There's a dull ache in my chest, and I remind myself we were a fling...nothing more.

# CHAPTER TEN

## BROOKS

My eyes pop open when the music in the entertainment tent starts, which I learn is exactly at seven. Way too early for partying in most places around the country, but this isn't just any city on any given day... This is Buxton, and it's race day.

I'm brushing my teeth when someone pounds on the door, and I nearly jump out of my skin. When I push the door open, Faith's standing there with her arms crossed. She's tapping her foot. Her eyes rake across my naked chest, and her tongue darts out, sweeping across her bottom lip and doing nothing to ease my morning wood.

She's dressed in a pair of black skinny jeans with a yellow and blue V-neck Ridley Racing T-shirt. The peaks of her breasts are clearly visible and glistening in the morning sunlight. I swear the woman is on this planet just to torture me and make me pay for some unspeakable crime I have no recollection of committing.

She finally looks at my face, and her eyes narrow because I'm smiling, soaking up the sight of her. "Why don't you put some clothes on? We're late."

"Want to come in?"

"No." Her tone's clipped, and I can tell she's still pissed at me about last night.

Faith tried more than once to get me to open up, but I couldn't. She wouldn't understand the enormity of her father calling me son. No one could ever understand unless they grew up the way I did. Instead of trying to explain how I felt, I pulled back and kept everything locked inside.

I wanted to explain everything to her, but Faith made it perfectly clear that keeping our distance would be best, and I couldn't argue with her decision.

"Please." I take a step back, motioning for her to follow. "We need to talk."

She glances around, smiling at the anxious fans as they walk by. "We don't have time."

I rest my hands on the doorframe and lean forward, hoping at least my body can entice her in. "I have something to say."

"Go, Brooks," a woman says, fist pumping the air as she passes by.

I give the nice lady a smile with a playful wink. Sally's her name. She is a part-time resident at the RV park but lives for this weekend and claims to be the biggest Ridley Racing fan in the small town.

Faith glares at the woman's back and waves her hand. "So, say it."

I raise an eyebrow. "You want me to say whatever I'm going to say in front of all these people?" She purses her lips as I raise an eyebrow. "I have no problem putting our business..."

I don't get the rest of the sentence out before Faith's body lurches forward. Her hand collides with my chest, pushing me inside the trailer as she slams the door behind her. "Shut up! Just shut your face."

Staying away from Faith, pretending that nothing happened between us, has been the hardest damn thing I've had to do in my entire life. I can't take another minute without her in my arms, pressing my lips against hers and stealing her sweet breath. Every ounce of restraint I've shown slips as I grab her wrist, pull her against my body, and cover her lips with mine.

She pushes against my chest as she tries to pull away. I slide one arm around her back, refusing to let her go so easily. "Don't," I murmur against her lips, loving how she feels pressed against my body.

She slides her tongue across my bottom lip with a soft moan, kissing me back and making my heart beat faster. When her hands slide up my arms and tangle in my hair, I tighten my hold and close the last bit of space between us. My head spins as our tongues tangle together, as if I'm almost drunk on the taste of her. I'm teasing myself. No, torturing is more fitting to describe the way her breasts press against my chest as she moans into my mouth.

The kiss isn't enough, and yet, it's everything.

I release her wrist and place my palm against her cheek, resting my thumb where our mouths have become one. With each passing second, I know I'm running out of time to tell her what I need to in order to have my head in the race.

Slowly, I pull my lips away from hers and open my eyes. "Faith," I whisper against her mouth. "We have to talk about us."

I'm ready for her to hit me. Prepared for her to storm out of the trailer without so much as a backward glance. Faith doesn't do either.

She drops her head, rests her forehead against my lips, and breathes heavily. "I can't, Brooks."

I kiss the soft skin near her hair, inhaling the sweet scent of her perfume, and close my eyes. "I need to tell you something before I go out there today." I grab her face, forcing her eyes to mine because I want her to not only hear what I have to say but feel the words too. "I'm sorry about last night at your parents'. I was an asshole."

"I know you were." The corner of her mouth rises.

"I've never been to a family dinner. You gotta remember, I didn't have a family. I barely had a mother, let alone anyone else. We never sat at a table, talking and eating, just enjoying being around everyone. It was overwhelming for me."

She blinks slowly and relaxes. "I'm sorry," she says, but I don't know what she has to be sorry about. I was the one who acted like a complete tool and shut her out.

"Earlier in the day, when your father invited me to dinner, he called me son." I pause when my nose starts to tingle. "Son," I repeat with wide eyes, and her eyebrows shoot up in recognition. "My own mother never even called me that."

Her bottom lip trembles. "I'm sorry," she says again.

"That wasn't just a dinner at your family's house. Your dad made me feel like I belong, and there's nothing I want more in the world than to be part of something bigger and better than just me. I never thought I cared much for having a family. I told myself I didn't care. I lied to myself, Faith. I want everything I never thought I could have."

"Of course you can have a family."

I shake my head. She isn't getting what I'm saying, but I haven't done the best job explaining the enormity of what I'm saying. "I don't want just any family. I want to be a part of yours."

"Oh," she squeaks.

Leaning my head forward, I rest my forehead against hers and peer through my lashes. "I want you so badly I ache, Faith. Staying away from you has been torture, and you shutting me out completely cut me to the core. But last night, surrounded by your family, I knew I couldn't spend another day without you."

"But..."

"No. Let me finish."

She nods.

"I want you. I want the Ridleys. I want everything. We can't sneak around anymore."

"Brooks." She flattens her palms against my chest but doesn't push me away.

"I can't keep lying to your dad, because being away from you is too much. If he kicks me off the team after this weekend, then so be it."

Her eyes grow as big as saucers and she gasps.

"You're worth risking everything."

This isn't just about her and me. This is the entire package. The family. The racing. The dynasty. Every little thing that has fallen into my lap recently makes me realize I want more. I want more than a racing title.

She pulls her face out of my grip and backs away, gawking at me. "Don't do something so foolish."

Her words are like a punch to the gut.

I step toward her, and she steps back. "It's not foolish. I can't stand the thought of having to pretend we're nothing for the entire season."

"Yesterday you could barely touch my hand, and today you're what...professing your love?"

"I wouldn't say love, princess, but I'm definitely addicted."

I've never been drawn to a person like I am her. Women came and went, just like my mother, and I never gave them another thought. But Faith...she's in my face, circling around every aspect of my life, and no matter how hard I try, resisting her hasn't been easy.

"You can't throw everything away because you like fucking me."

I growl. "I'm not throwing anything away because I like fucking you, Faith. I'm willing to give everything up for a chance at something real."

She squares her shoulder and stiffens. "This isn't real, Brooks. It was just sex. You were a good lay and nothing more."

I take another step forward, closing the small amount of space between us, and wrap my hand around her upper arm. I grind my teeth together, trying to tamper down the rage that's building inside me. She's lying. I can see it in her eyes. "Take that back. You can't kiss me like you just did and tell me we're nothing."

Her gaze dips to my hand before narrowing. She slowly turns her head and looks me straight in the eyes. "If you know what's good for you, you'll remove your hand, get dressed, and get your ass to the track." She lifts her hands and peels my fingers away from her skin. "I'm your boss, Brooks. I was drunk when we had sex."

"The first time," I blurt out and can't stop myself from saying the words.

She pokes me in the chest, stabbing my skin with her fingernail. "Don't you dare tell my daddy we slept together. He'll murder you, and if he doesn't, I will."

I throw my hands up, knowing I'll never get her to see the light. "Fine." I grab a T-shirt out of the cabinet and lift my chin toward the door. "You coming with me?"

"You ready?"

"Yep." I nod and pull the shirt over my head as she storms out.

Faith can lie all she wants, but we both know the truth.

*She wants this as much as I do.*

I'm not going to stop until I get her to admit that my feelings aren't a one-way street.

## FAITH

My ears are already ringing, and the race hasn't even started. The latest country hit is blasting through the speakers and echoing across the infield. I cover my eyes, squinting as I glance around the grandstands. They're filled earlier than usual, and so many are sporting Ridley Racing yellow and blue, showing support for their hometown team.

"You ready for this?" my dad asks Brooks after Roscoe heads to his car.

Brooks drags his fingers across the hood, unable to tear his eyes away from the shiny blue paint. "I am, sir. I've never been more ready for anything in my whole life."

"Kick some ass out there. I'll be on the radio along with the crew chief, and we'll be with you every step of the way. If she doesn't feel right, let us know right away so we can bring you into pit road."

Brooks nod and taps his fingers against the hood. "I got it."

My dad takes a step forward and squeezes Brooks's shoulder as he stares him straight in the eyes. "Follow your instincts, son. Do your best to qualify for tomorrow's main event."

Brooks's hard stare changes. "I'll do my best to make you proud."

My father gives him a chin lift. "Now get your ass in that car and drive like the devil."

Brooks laughs and grabs his helmet off the tool chest next to him. "Buxton won't know what hit 'em." He glances my way and smiles.

My lips tingle as the memory of our earlier kiss comes flooding back. I want to tell him I'm sorry and I didn't mean a single word I said earlier, but I can't. My father's standing next to him, waiting for him to move his ass.

"Good luck," I say quickly.

Brooks's smile widens, and he opens his mouth to say something but snaps his lips closed.

My father claps his hands together and ruins whatever moment we were about to have. "The race is going to start without ya, kid."

"Sorry," Brooks says before turning back toward his waiting number thirteen.

My entire body tingles as Brooks holds his head high, helmet in one hand, dressed head to toe in Ridley blue and looking every bit a champion. I trace the curve of my lips with my finger as he slides into his car like he's done the maneuver a thousand times before.

"This is it," Dad says, slipping his arm across my shoulders and pulling me close. "We have two boys to cheer on today. You ready for this?"

I peer up at him and smile. "I'm always ready for race day, Daddy."

The one thing I'm not ready for is to admit I'm slowly falling for a race car driver. I swore them off long ago and told myself I'd never get involved. But that was before Brooks, with his sexy grin and sweet Southern charm, started getting under my skin.

"Drivers, start your engines," the announcer says over the loud speaker.

Dad releases me and fist pumps the air. "It's race day, baby!" he hollers, and I jump, not expecting him to be so excited.

I grab a set of headphones from the tool chest and weave my way out of the pit area as the engines roar to life. The ground below me shakes as the crowd rises to their feet and waves their hands in the air. I cover my ears when the sound becomes too much, so I hear nothing but my daddy, the pit chief, Roscoe, and Brooks for the rest of the race.

The pace car comes up on the side of pit road as the drivers rev their engines, and I find a seat next to Mamma. She turns to me and smiles, but we don't bother with words because we're both too nervous and can't hear each other anyway.

My heart's practically in my throat as Brooks pulls out, following the cars in front of him and heading onto the field. The cars weave side to side, warming their tires before the race.

"Remember, if you're going to take the bottom line, do it early," Daddy tells the boys through the headphones. "Brooks, try to get out of traffic as fast as possible and protect Roscoe."

There's a grunt, but I don't know if it's Brooks not liking what he hears or Roscoe reveling in those very words. My hand tightens on my knee, trying to stop my legs from shaking uncontrollably. I've never been this crazy when Roscoe raced, not even the first time, but with Brooks...there's something different there.

I hold my breath as the cars near the starting line, waiting for the green flag to wave. Brooks's car jerks to the right, almost crashing into the orange car next to him.

"Son, it's a long race. Don't give me a heart attack before the damn thing starts."

"Just psyching him out, sir."

"Save it for the race," Daddy tells him, and I can hear the amusement in his voice.

I can barely breathe as the pace car pulls onto pit road and the green flag waves wildly through the air. My entire body trembles as the cars speed by turn one, right in front of my seat. I jump up and down, screaming for Brooks as he blazes by in a blur. The laps are quick on the short half-mile track. There's no relaxing or time to settle at Buxton. There's less than fifteen seconds to each lap and four tight turns with a helluva bank. The drivers lay on the gas in the straight, trying to pull ahead as they peel out of the turn.

I gasp as Brooks bumps the car in front of him as they begin the second lap. My mother grabs my wrist, sharing every bit of my anxiety. I swallow the lump that's hanging in my throat when he doesn't spin out of control and give my mother a tight smile.

Shaking my hands, I try to control my breathing, because at this rate, I'll hyperventilate and pass out before the race is even halfway done.

"How's she handling?" the crew chief says over the headphones.

"Like a beaut," Brooks replies.

"She's handling well," Roscoe says.

"Find the rhythm."

"We know," Roscoe says in an irritated voice. "Let us drive."

There's nothing more to say. Not this early in the race. I glance at the jumbotron as I settle back into my seat. Only four hundred and ninety-seven more laps of agony to go.

# CHAPTER ELEVEN

## BROOKS

"How many more?" I ask, knowing we're close to the end.

The wheel jerks back and forth even as I tighten my grip, trying to keep her going where she needs to be headed. So far, the race has gone as planned, and I haven't managed to demolish my car into a million little pieces like Roscoe had predicted.

"Five. What's wrong?" Beau asks, and I can hear the panic.

"Just making sure I don't run out of gas."

The car feels like a toaster even on this mild spring day because of the engine blowing back heat into the cabin and no air conditioning. Sweat is dripping from every pore of my body, and my muscles ache like I'm running a marathon. I curse under my breath as I whip around turn four and narrowly miss the wall.

"That's affirmative. You're good to go," the pit chief replies.

"Just calm down, son. You're doing great. Push her harder," Beau says like I haven't already been pushing the hell out of the car and keeping my focus on the race.

The car trembles underneath me, almost fighting me at every turn, but I keep control. The track's covered in rubber, pulling from the tires and increasing the grip of the tires like glue. That's something I never experienced on a dirt track.

"After the next turn, power by the guy in front of you."

That's easy for him to say. I've been trying to blow past the guy for the last three laps, but he hasn't given me an inch. There's two cars ahead of me. Roscoe's leading the pack but barely. Number twenty-two is hot on his tail. When I go up, twenty-two follows. When I head down, so does he. When I try to pull in front of him, he comes right at me.

"Bump 'im," Roscoe says, giving me an open invitation to do what I've been wanting to for the last ten minutes.

"Happily." I lay my foot on the gas, gearing up for the next turn, and hold my breath.

I slide up the bank and twenty-two follows, but at the last second, I cut the wheel, grazing his bumper. He swerves, heading up the bank as I fly past. I glance in my rearview mirror, catching a glimpse as his car spins down, heading toward the infield.

"Yes!" Roscoe cheers as twenty-two is down for the count, leaving Ridley Racing at the top.

"Fucker deserved that," I say.

The caution lights flash, and the pace car enters the track in front of Roscoe. The last two laps of the race go at a snail's pace as they clean up the debris from twenty-two's car that scattered across the track.

"We got this, boys!" Beau yells, almost blasting out my eardrums. "Tomorrow's going to be a great day."

"Good race, Brooks." Roscoe swerves back and forth in front of me, following the pace car over the finish line. The checkered flag waves overhead, and the race is officially over.

Roscoe speeds away, sticking an arm out the window and feeding the frenzy from the grandstand. I take a deep breath, finally filling my lungs with air for the first time since the green flag waved. My muscles relax as relief washes over me, and I know there will never be another race like it. Everything about today was different than being on dirt. There's a finesse to the asphalt I hadn't experienced. No amount of practice, even with Roscoe at my side, could've prepared me for today.

I wrap my hand around the window frame as I slide out, knowing my knees are going to be like jelly and will try to buckle underneath me.

Mr. Ridley grabs my helmet with both hands, pulling me upright. "You did it. I knew you'd be a beast out there."

I don't know what to say. I can't talk. I'm too overcome with every emotion as the adrenaline starts to wear off. The reality slams into me. I finished my first pro race and came in second to the reigning champion. I only needed a few more laps, and I could've beaten Roscoe too. I know that, and I'm sure it's in the back of his mind as he takes his victory lap, eating up the excitement from the hometown fans.

"This is going to be a damn fine season. Damn fine, I tell ya," Mr. Ridley says and hugs me tightly.

I lose my breath as tears form in my eyes. The emotion crashes over me in waves, building with each passing second. I don't pull away, letting him embrace me as if I were the kid in the winner's circle I'd dreamed so many times of being.

Mr. Ridley releases me and slaps my shoulder, but I keep my balance. "Take that helmet off before you pass out. It's hotter than a billy goat with a blow torch out here."

I pull off my helmet and laugh. God, I love Mr. Ridley. I'll never be able to repay him for taking a chance on me and giving me a shot when probably nobody else would.

"Did the race scramble your brain?"

I peer up at him, squinting as the sun blazes behind his head. "No, sir."

He gives me a quick nod. "Good. Team meeting after the race to prep for tomorrow. I'm going to find Roscoe. You coming?"

"No, sir. I'm going to write down some notes, and then I'm all yours."

The racer life isn't easy. People always assume we drive around in circles and there isn't much else to the entire thing, but that's the furthest from the truth. We spend hours prepping, tuning the cars between races, testing out changes to the engine and fittings under the hood, trying to make the car faster and better for the next race. There's barely any downtime. Thirty-eight weeks on the road, and we hit every major track in the country. I imagine by the time it's all over, I'm going to feel like a used dishrag, but nothing worth having ever comes easy or without working my ass off.

"Hey," Faith says behind my back as her father heads toward Roscoe.

I spin around, wanting nothing more than to pull her into my arms and celebrate. Her mother is at her side, but she's smiling at least. "Hey." I lift my chin, deciding to keep my hands as close to my body as possible.

"You did wonderful out there, Brooks." Mrs. Ridley lifts

her sunglasses and slides them back into her long auburn hair with a small smile.

"Thank you, ma'am." I let my gaze drift between Faith and Mrs. Ridley.

They could be twins except for the few lines near Mrs. Ridley's eyes. The resemblance is uncanny and undeniable. It's like looking into the future, seeing what Faith will look like in twenty years, and I gotta say...she may be a bigger knockout than she already is.

"The way you hit twenty-two..." Faith's voice drifts and her eyes widen.

"Pretty damn cool, huh?" I grin, proud of how everything turned out. One wrong move, another inch to the right, and we both could've very well been heading into the wall in a cloud of smoke.

"I forgot how to breathe for a moment."

Her words make my easy grin slide into a full-blown smile. So damn big, my cheeks start to ache because Faith just clued me in on something even if she didn't mean. She can say we're nothing and that we only fooled around a few times, but she cares. No one's going to hold their breath unless they're scared.

Mrs. Ridley peers down at her daughter. "We were both worried. After the meeting tonight, come over for dinner. I want to make sure you're well-nourished for tomorrow's race. There's a lot at stake."

"Yes, ma'am."

"Mimi." She smiles.

"Yes, Mimi. I'll be there."

"Seven sharp."

I nod and know last time I almost screwed the pooch by knocking on the door with only moments to spare. I was so nervous to walk into that house, surrounded by a family, to do something I'd never done before. This time will be different. The conversation will be easier, the feelings a little less overwhelming, and maybe it'll be the perfect time to talk to Mr. Ridley about his daughter.

Mrs. Ridley walks away, and Faith pulls on my uniform. "I can see your wheels spinning inside that head. Whatever you're thinking...don't."

"Princess," I say with a smirk, and she yanks my sleeve out of frustration.

"Brooks." There's warning in her voice, but I've never been good at listening.

"Let me worry about what's going on in my head. We both know you're falling in love with me."

Her eyes narrow and her lips tighten. "I hate you."

"Denial is the first step." I wink.

"I can't deal with you right now. I have work to do," she says before marching away from me in long angry strides.

My feet don't move as I watch her walk away, those beautiful lush hips swaying, calling to me. I love seeing her a little worked up. There's a fire in her. One I want. One I need to be a part of, and I won't stop until she says the words I want to hear.

♦ ♦ ♦ ♦

Hours pass before I make the walk back to my trailer after the team meeting. My body wants to collapse and get some much-needed sleep, but the rest of me is all about going to the Ridleys' and seeing Faith. My shoulders are pushed back and my head held high as I weave my way through the crowd of people partying in the courtyard of the RV park.

Racing fans stop me every few feet, recognizing my face from the jumbotron at the track, and congratulate me on my first race. I smile, sign a few autographs, and soak up every bit of their excitement. There's not a damn thing that could ruin my mood, not even Faith's denial.

"Way to go, Brooks!" someone yells across the courtyard, and I wave in their direction.

"A woman's waiting for you," Maud, the trailer park resident gossip, says just as my hand touches the door handle to my place.

"Who?" I freeze and turn my head toward Maud and the other small group of campers sitting next door.

"I don't know, but I never figured you for the older woman type." Her eyes rake over me with a wicked smile. "I would've tried my hand at you if I'd known."

Older woman? I have nothing against them, but I haven't been with an older woman—at least one who clearly appears to be older—since high school.

My heart pounds wildly as I pull open the door and step inside.

"Hey, baby." The voice stops me in my tracks.

I close my eyes as the blood drains from my face. I take a deep breath, knowing I can't make a scene because Maud and the rest of the residents would eat that shit up. "What are you doing here?"

My mother unfolds herself from the couch and walks toward me. "I couldn't miss your first big race."

I back away before she can touch me. "You're not welcome here."

Her brows furrow, but she doesn't stop. "Don't act like that. I'm your momma."

I laugh and shake my head. "You gave birth to me, but not once in my life have you actually been a mother."

Even now, standing in my trailer on one of the biggest days of my life, she's a mess. She's drunk. I don't need to get any closer to her to see the signs written plain as day. The entire trailer reeks of alcohol, and from the looks of her, she hasn't been sober in a very long time. The bags around her eyes are more pronounced and darker than I remember. Her hair is filled with knots, almost matted against the side of her head.

"Baby." The word slides off her tongue like she's been calling me that my whole life. She takes two more steps toward me, and I swallow down the anger, trying to get my ass in check before something bad happens. "Aren't you a little happy to see me?"

My head jerks back and my eyes widen. "Are you serious?"

The absurdity of the entire thing is beyond comprehension. She's been missing from my life for years, not even so much as a phone call on my birthday or Christmas, and never gave a shit if I was alive or dead. But now...with me joining the pro circuit, she has dollar signs in her eyes.

She places her hand on my chest, staring up with a grin. "Can't a momma love her child?"

I wrap my hand around her wrist and peel her fingers

away from my body. "You've never been a mother. I'm only going to say this once. You're not welcome in my life. Don't follow me around the country. Don't ask me for any favors. You're nothing to me."

Her eyes flash as her lips snarl. Where hurt should be, there's only anger. She's not here to love me. She didn't show up to check to see if I was okay. The woman only wants money to buy more booze and drugs, losing a little more of herself and feeding the addiction that's had her for over twenty years.

I tighten my hold on her wrist when she tries to slap me in the face. "If you want to go to rehab and get help, I'll pay for it. You need or want anything else, forget I exist."

The door to my trailer opens. "I didn't..." Faith says but doesn't finish the statement.

*Fuck.* I turn, releasing my mother's hand, and move toward Faith. The position I was in, holding my mother's arm with barely any space between us could look shady to anyone. The last person I wanted to see me in this situation, or meet my mother, just walked through the door.

Faith steps back and pushes open the door with her ass. "I'm sorry."

"No. Wait."

"Always the ladies' man, Brooks," my mother says, clearly not knowing when she isn't welcome and doing everything in her power to insert herself in my life.

"It's not what you think," I blurt out, reaching for Faith before she can step outside.

Her eyes are locked on mine, and I can see the hurt in Faith's eyes. "I shouldn't have come here," she says before running out the door without so much as looking back or letting me explain.

"Don't shed any tears over that one, Brooks. A rich girl like her would never really love a guy like you."

In that moment, with my mother showing her true colors, I decide to do something I swore I'd never do... I'm going to introduce the Ridleys to my version of family.

## FAITH

"Brooks is late," my father says as he glances down at his watch for the third time.

We're standing in the dining room, each of us behind our chairs with the food already on the table. My mom doesn't want anyone to sit until the final person has arrived. It's some weird custom she has, and until now, there's never been an issue.

My mom wraps her hands around the back of the chair until her knuckles turn white. "Anyone hear from him this evening?"

"He called earlier. An old friend stopped by to see him," I lie.

I'm riddled with guilt by the way I ran out on him, but I couldn't stand there in the presence of another woman and keep my cool. The way they were standing, almost pressed together as he held her arm. They were more than casual acquaintances.

My dad touches my mother's hand as soon as there's a knock on the door. "I'll get it."

No one says anything as he leaves the dining room.

Roscoe's too busy staring at the food to care about anything much besides stuffing his face, and I'm too angry to bother with small talk.

"Son. Who's this?"

*No. Freaking. Way.* He wouldn't dare bring her to my parents' house. There's a sudden burning sensation in my throat I can't swallow away. Why on earth Brooks would bring someone else to our family dinner is beyond me. I thought he was a normal guy, but once again...I was wrong.

My father walks in first, followed by Brooks and the cheap floozy from the trailer. Roscoe's eyes widen as he catches sight of the tramp traipsing through our dining room. I wrinkle my nose, trying to not throw up from the smell of alcohol and filth that seeps from her pores and fills the room.

"I knew you lied about liking older women after what happened with Ms. Constance, but dude..." Roscoe scratches his jaw and laughs. "I never would've expected this."

*What happened with Constance?*

"Sit down and be quiet," my daddy tells Roscoe.

"Who do we have here, Brooks?" my mother asks, somehow maintaining a smile.

My gaze slices to Brooks as he stands next to the woman wearing very little clothing and looking every bit a streetwalker. I hold myself back when all I want to do is march up to him and slap him across the face. How dare he bring her into my childhood home, throwing his sexual exploits in my face. She's nothing special. If he's trying to make me jealous, he isn't, but my stomach's rolling, and every butterfly I'd ever had disintegrates.

“This is Jane.” He pauses, and I narrow my gaze, throwing tiny little daggers at him with my eyes. “My mother.”

I start to stagger back and grab on to my chair for support. Brooks drops his hands to his side, and I turn my face, unable to look at him. I may have gotten the wrong idea about him and his mother, but there’s no denying the words Roscoe just uttered, not knowing Brooks and I had a...whatever you want to call what happened between us.

The last two words echo in my mind, and the entire situation now makes complete sense. Everything clicks as I turn my eyes to Jane, the very drunk and complete mess at his side. My eyes go wide, and I know I was a total asshole and jumped to conclusions about what was going on inside the trailer when I showed up unannounced.

Jane sways a little as she stands at his side. There’s a blank spot where one of her front teeth used to be, but she still cracks a smile, not the least bit embarrassed. “Damn. This is a mighty fine place you have,” she says instead of saying hello. Her eyes are roaming the room, taking in the antiques that line a buffet table near the front window.

Brooks is staring at me, and his jaw ticks. He’s angry, but I’m not sure if he’s mad at his mother or at me for running off earlier.

My mother walks around the table and never takes her eyes off Jane. “Why, Ms. Carter, it’s wonderful to meet you.”

I may have my mother’s looks, but her ability to be charming in every situation didn’t rub off on me. If I were in her shoes, I’d be walking the woman who’s clearly eyeing the expensive items right out of the house, but not my mamma.

Jane gawks as my mother extends her hand but doesn't take it. "And you are?"

"I'm Mrs. Ridley."

Jane purses her lips, giving my mother a once-over. "Lucky lady with the fancy house and handsome husband," she says as Brooks covers his face and shakes his head. "I could've had all that too."

"I'm sorry, Mimi, but I wanted to come in person and tell you that I'm unable to eat with you tonight. I appreciate you thinking of me, but I have my mother to tend to."

"Don't be silly, boy. Look at all this food, and I'm starving," his mother says, slurring her words when she speaks.

Moving the chair out, I sit down and keep my back to them. I feel awful about his mother and the embarrassment of having her come around at an important time like this, but the other part of me wants to smack him straight in the face. How dare he pretend he wants me and that we were more than a cheap fling when he slept with Constance too.

"Let's go, Mother. We're done bothering these nice people."

"But..."

"Let's go," he says with more harshness to his voice. "Thank you, Mr. and Mrs. Ridley."

I haven't moved. I'm facing Roscoe, watching him shovel food in his mouth like he's never eaten before. My heart's broken, shattered in a million tiny pieces over a guy who isn't even mine to begin with.

I know getting mixed up with a race car driver is foolish. I've spent too much time around them. I know they have wandering eyes and hands. I'd never settle for a relationship where my man isn't one hundred percent committed to me, and that includes Brooks Carter.

# CHAPTER TWELVE

**FAITH**

I plop down on the couch and drop my head onto the pillow behind me. “How could I have been so stupid?” I’m talking to myself. Something I do more often lately.

I barely ate dinner, much to my mother’s dismay. I couldn’t stop thinking about Brooks and Constance. Although my mother didn’t say anything, she kept glancing at me with a tight, pained smile. I’m the one who pushed them together. Me and my big, dumb idea. But how was I supposed to know I’d like Brooks? I’d never liked any driver on the circuit. Well, except Tommy Bows because he winked at me, but I was a naïve seventeen-year-old.

My head snaps forward as soon as I hear heavy footsteps in the stairwell. I’m on my feet and running toward the door, stubbing my pinky toe on the coffee table on the way. I hop on one foot, swearing and gasping for air as I hold my toe and try to balance.

“Faith.”

I plaster my back to the door and try to find my breath. “Go away,” I say, barely getting the words out.

There’s a loud thump against the door, but I don’t move.

"Please," he begs. "We gotta talk."

I inhale and rub the ache from my toe. "Fuck off, Brooks. There's nothing to talk about."

"Let me explain."

My body jerks forward as he hits the door again.

"I'm going to smack my head until you let me in or I give myself a concussion."

I'm not letting him in. There's no way I'm going to let him sweet talk me with a string of lies. There's no covering up what happened. After dinner, I cornered Roscoe and made him spill the details. My stomach turned as he told me what Constance had said about her evening with the new boy. She didn't tell Roscoe, but he heard it through the Buxton grapevine because nothing stays secret for long in this little town.

"Talk through the door. You're not coming inside."

I do not care if my dad gets mad because Brooks shows up tomorrow with a knot the size of a baseball sticking out of his forehead. There's no way I'm letting him inside to work his hot man voodoo on me.

"I'm sorry about my mom. I told you she was a drunk and an asshole."

I cross my arms over my chest and turn around to face the door, giving it the same shitty look I would give him if he were in the room. "I'm sorry about your mom, Brooks. Really I am. I'm not upset about her."

There's a long pause, and I think I've said enough to send him on his way.

"Then open the damn door. I need to see you." There's silence again, and I step toward the door, thinking he's leaving.

"No. Fuck that. I want to see you."

He wants to see me? I don't give a crap what he wants. I wanted to fall for a normal guy. Maybe someone who didn't work in the racing industry and didn't have a clue who my dad was or the kind of money I grew up around. But nope. That would've made my life too easy. "Why don't you go see Constance," I blurt out.

"Constance?" I can hear shock in his voice, but I don't believe him.

He knows exactly what I'm talking about. He never even talked about his date with her. Just glossed over the entire evening, telling me how she was a nice lady and totally misunderstood. I take a step toward the door with my fists clenched at my side. "If you're looking for a warm body, I'm sure Constance would be more than happy to keep you company tonight," I say bitterly.

"Fuck," he mutters and hits his head harder this time. "I don't know what the hell you're talking about. Constance is just a friend."

"We're friends too," I remind him. "We've fucked, in case you forgot." I cringe, hoping my neighbors didn't hear that. If they did, I'm sure it'll get back to my mother before too long. "Just go, Brooks. Whatever happened between you and Constance is none of my business."

"But it is your business, Faith."

I lean forward and place my forehead against the door. Why does my heart have to hurt so bad? I can't keep doing this, especially with the long season with us both on the road together. My heart can't take this. "Just go home, Brooks.

Leave me alone."

"Not until you tell me what the hell you mean about Constance. I didn't even touch the woman."

We're still talking through the door, and I want nothing more than to rip the damn thing open and see his face. Watch him squirm as I throw the truth out there, but I don't dare. "That's not what she said."

"She's a liar, Faith. You know how she is. Nothing happened."

I close my eyes and lean my entire weight against the door. "I don't believe you."

"I can't believe you're going to believe Constance over me."

"I don't even know you."

"But you do know Constance. Who do you think is telling the truth?"

His words are like a punch to the gut. I don't know what to believe anymore. I've known Constance my entire life, and she's never been one for the truth. She's never been an honorable person. I know better than to believe the gossip coming down the pipeline in Buxton, but I don't really know Brooks, even if I want to think I do.

I push off the door and start to pace. "Just go home. Tomorrow's a new day and the big race. We'll start over again and figure out how to be friends."

"What if I don't want to start over?"

I shake my head and glance up at the ceiling, wondering how I got myself into this mess. *He's hot and you were horny.* I should've known there was going to be a hefty price for letting my libido do the thinking and leading me astray.

"If we're going to work together, we have to at least learn to be friends," I say, figuring that's the best thing for both of us.

"Faith, I don't want friends."

"You've made that quite obvious!" I throw my hands up in disgust and shorten my strides, turning every few feet and following the same path.

"You don't understand," he says in a soft and gentle tone.

"I do. I got the message loud and clear."

"I want to be more than your friend, Faith. I want it more than anything in the world. I can't lie to your father anymore. You'll never understand because you've always had a dad in your life. I was going to tell him tonight. Did you know that? If I wanted to be your friend, do you honestly think I'd risk everything I've worked so hard to achieve?"

"I don't know, Brooks. I barely know you." I stop walking and stare at the door.

"For the first time, I felt like someone truly cared about me. Not just because of what I could do for them but because they like me."

"My daddy has a soft spot for you," I tell him, but I leave out the part that I do too.

There's something about Brooks that sucked me in from the moment I saw him, and I haven't been able to shake it. I still could've strangled him five minutes ago, but now...I don't know what to feel about the guy.

"He's not going to like me much when I tell him I'm falling in love with his daughter."

My eyes widen, and I cover my mouth with my hands.

*Brooks is falling in love with me?* I can't believe he just said those words and into a door instead of to my face. "You're what?" I ask because maybe I didn't quite hear him right with the whooshing of blood through my ears.

"Open the door, Faith."

## BROOKS

"Hey," she whispers as she cracks the door so I can see only one side of her face.

I'm leaning against the doorframe and trying to be cool. "Hey."

She doesn't say anything else. She's just staring at me with one green eye hidden behind the door. I want to rush inside, scoop her into my arms, and steal her breath in a kiss, but I don't want to ruin the moment. "I'm falling for you," I say. And then I repeat it. These are the words she needs to hear so she can break apart this wall she's built around herself to keep me out.

"You can't."

I place my hand against the door but don't push my way inside. "Let me in."

"I don't think it's a good idea."

"I miss you." I step forward and shove the door open. "I miss us." Faith lets go of the handle and walks backward as I step inside. "I can't keep doing what we're doing. I want you, princess. More than I've ever wanted anything before."

She stops moving and stares up at me with her big, beautiful eyes.

I close the space between us and slide my hand against

her cheek. “I want you so badly my chest hurts. Being with you is the closest I’ve come to pure absolute happiness.” Her eyes widen, but I don’t give her time to answer. “I can’t go on ignoring you. I can’t pretend nothing happened. I can’t stop the knot in my stomach when you walk out of a room or the butterflies that fill my insides when I see your face.”

“Brooks.” Her voice cracks. Faith presses her hand against my chest but doesn’t push me away.

I lean forward, bringing my lips close to hers, and want nothing more than to kiss her. “Don’t make me leave.”

Her gaze dips to my mouth. “I can’t.”

“I need you, Faith,” I admit, and saying the words isn’t as hard as I imagined. I’ve always been the type who never needed anyone, even as a kid. I learned to fly solo and keep myself busy, but after being with Faith, I couldn’t stomach the thought of being alone again. Wrapping an arm around her waist, I press her body against mine.

She slides her hand up my arm. “Kiss me.”

My eyes do not leave hers as I close the space between our mouths. Tightening my grip, I fuse my lips to hers. I drink her in, soaking up every smell and taste as she moans into my mouth and tangles her fingers in my hair. There’s something so perfect about the way she kisses me, like she craves my touch just as much as I crave hers. I slide my hand down and cup her ass, squeezing it gently in my palm. I’m lost in Faith, drowning in her.

“What the hell?” a familiar voice says from behind me.

I freeze, and my eyes fly open to find Faith’s panicked eyes staring back at me.

*Oh fuck.*

This isn't how I wanted tonight to go down. Hell, this isn't how I wanted our relationship outed. The last person in the world I wanted to first find out about Faith and me is Roscoe, but here he is standing behind me, probably ready to pounce.

I release my hold on Faith and turn to face her brother and explain myself. "It's not what it looks like."

His nostrils are flaring, and his hands are balled in fists at his side. "It looked like you were kissing my sister." There's no amusement in his voice. No smile on his face. The hatred I saw coming from him when I first hit town is nothing compared to the murderous look he's sporting now.

Faith grips my wrist and steps around me, putting herself in the line of fire. "Roscoe. Calm down. It was innocent."

A vein running down the middle of Roscoe's forehead pops as his shoulders bunch and his lips flatten. He hasn't taken his eyes off me, even with Faith standing in front of him. "There's nothing innocent about the way he was touching you."

She takes another step toward him and places her hand on his chest. "Okay. So, it was just what it looked like, but it is not what you think."

Roscoe's eyes dip to Faith for only a second before coming back to me. "This is between me and Brooks."

Besides being head over heels in love with his sister, there's one other thing I know for sure: I'm not getting out of this apartment without Roscoe laying hands on me. There's nothing that can be said to defuse the situation or alleviate his anger. Not only was I manhandling her, we lied to him about it, hiding it behind his back.

Faith shoves him backward with her hand. "This is none of your business, Roscoe. I'm an adult. Brooks is an adult. What we do has nothing to do with you."

"Like hell," he growls. "Move, Faith."

Roscoe grips her below her shoulders and lifts her into the air before setting her to the side like she's a decoration. "You're a real motherfucker. You're going to pay for this!" Roscoe yells and charges at me. His fist is already pulled back, ready to strike as soon as he's within range.

I've never had a sister. I don't know what the rules are when it comes to shit like this. Do I stand here and let him beat me to a pulp to get his anger out so we can deal with the situation like men, or do I charge forward and fight back?

In a split second, I stand my ground, not backing up or rushing forward, and wait for his attack. He moves fast, hurling his fist through the air with so much rage in his eyes I should be scared, but I'm not.

My head snaps back as soon as his fist connects with my jaw, and my bones crunch under the pressure. Pain radiates across my face as I right myself. I don't wait for the next blow. I see it coming. He already has his hand in the air, but I duck at the last second, making him miss.

"Let's talk about this like men," I say and rub the pain from my jaw.

"A man would've said something to me before trying to take my sister to bed."

There was no way in hell I'd ever tell him I already had. What he walked in on was nothing compared to the things we did after the bar.

"Stop!" Faith yells, trying to come between us again, but Roscoe pushes her out of the way without even looking at her.

"Touch her again, and we're going to have a bigger problem," I warn him. She may be his sister, but I'll happily lay him out for putting his hands on her. No man, not even me, has a reason to touch a woman that way, especially not Faith.

My words set him off again as he moves toward me with more determination than before. Before he has a chance to pull his fist back, I step forward and slam my knuckles under his jaw. His body lurches backward as he stumbles to find his footing. "Want more?" I taunt. I'm ready to do this until he gets it out of his system, because there's no way in hell I'm leaving Faith alone or cutting her out of my life.

Faith jumps in her brother's face, poking him in the chest with the tip of her finger. "Get the hell out of my apartment before I call the police," she hisses.

His eyes narrow. "You wouldn't dare."

She squares her shoulders and leans forward. "Try me, brother."

He holds his jaw in his palm and glares at me over her head. "This shit is not over."

"Leave," Faith says, pointing at the doorway and not moving.

Roscoe stares at me and growls before he takes a few steps back toward the open door. He cracks his knuckles and laughs like a psycho. "Wait until Daddy hears about this, Miss Priss. He's going to lose his shit," he says before turning his back and jogging down the stairs.

If he's anything like Roscoe, I think he's going to run me

over with the race car he spent months fixing up just for me. Probably criss-cross my body more than once at maximum speed and still not feel satisfied afterward.

I place my hands on Faith's arms and hold her. "I'm sorry, Faith."

She turns to face me, on the verge of tears as her bottom lip trembles. Her eyes skate across my face, taking in the damage. "Jesus," she whispers and touches my cheek.

I wince but try to play everything off. "It's not as bad as it looks."

"Uh-huh." There's a hint of a smile on her face. "Just like us kissing wasn't exactly what it looked like."

I brush my mouth against hers as lightly as possible because my jaw feels like it's on fire. "I better go. I don't want your daddy finding me here tonight."

She sighs as her shoulders sag. "I don't want you to leave. He's not going to tell my father anything. At least not tonight. Roscoe needs you in that race tomorrow. Afterward"—she grimaces—"all bets are off."

"Great," I groan, knowing my day of reckoning is coming.

# CHAPTER THIRTEEN

## BROOKS

One of the crew looks up from the hood of my car and catches sight of my bruises. "What the hell happened to your face?"

I spent all night icing the damn thing to avoid swelling and bruising, but it was a losing battle. No amount of concealer I'd borrowed from Maud could cover the red and purple marks from the bottom of my jaw to my cheek. "Nothing," I say and turn my face away from him.

"Who's the girl?" he replies with a whimsical smile.

I pull the brim of my hat down and keep walking, ignoring him entirely. So far, I have been able to avoid Mr. Ridley, but I know he is not too far away. Roscoe's probably already ratted me out, and chances are I will be off the team immediately after today's race.

"Brooks!" Mr. Ridley yells in the distance. I freeze and think about hightailing it in the other direction. "Get your ass over here."

My stomach sinks when I see Roscoe standing next to him with his arms crossed, glaring at me. The little prick ratted on me. I know he said something because he couldn't be a man and let me tell his father first. Walking in their direction, I stare at the ground as an enormous knot forms in the pit of my stomach and bile rises in my throat.

"Let me see your face," Mr. Ridley says when I'm only a few feet away.

I close my eyes and take a deep breath, waiting for the words that will inevitably come from his lips. Slowly, I lift my eyes to his and brace myself for what comes next.

He clicks his tongue against the roof of his mouth and shakes his head as his eyes roam around my face. "I don't know what happened last night between the two of you, but leave it off the track. You got me?"

"Yes, sir." I nod with confusion as my eyes flicker to Roscoe.

"I don't give a shit if you two want to beat the hell out of each other, but don't mess with the team. You hear me?"

"Yes, Dad," Roscoe says, glaring at me.

"We'll figure this mess out later. You two need to be able to work together. I can't have you beating the piss out of one another and jeopardizing our entire season. I want you to keep it clean out there and bring home a title. Don't bring your personal shit into my cars."

"Yes, sir," I repeat.

"We won't." Roscoe's eyes don't leave mine.

"Shake hands like men." Mr. Ridley dips his chin and looks between the two of us.

Neither of us move until Mr. Ridley crosses his arms and grumbles. We shake, but nothing about it is comfortable or natural.

"Now go get ready. We have a race to win. You're

teammates, and you'd better damn well start acting like it, for Christ's sake."

I'm in shock and confused as Roscoe mutters something under his breath and walks away. I would've bet everything I owned on the fact Roscoe would run straight to his dad and tell him everything, but I don't think he did. I'm sure he's waiting for the perfect moment, but he actually surprised me.

Pulling my hat back down, I head toward the company trailer to change into my suit and prep for the long race ahead of me. I got to get my head in the race and focus all my energy on winning—or at least trying like hell to beat Roscoe and not think about what's going to happen afterward. Whether or not I have a future on this team, today's race is more important than any I've ever driven before. Once Mr. Ridley finds out, I need to make sure I'm not expendable or easily replaced.

"Does he know?" Faith asks as soon as I close the door, and I nearly trip backward.

"Damn, girl." I clutch my chest and exhale. I've already had enough stress thrown at me this morning that Faith's little ninja act only makes things worse. "You scared the shit out of me."

She pushes off the couch and walks toward me, looking petrified. "Does he know?"

I shake my head. "No. I don't think Roscoe told him."

Her eyes widen. "You sure about that?"

"Yep. Your dad doesn't know anything besides Roscoe and I have matching bruises. But he made us promise whatever shit went down stays off the track."

Faith laughs, tipping her head backward as her red hair

cascades over her shoulders. "Roscoe is not going to let it go so easy. He's going to try to bury you today."

"Should I let him win?" The thought alone makes me sick, but this is not only my livelihood, this is Faith's family.

"Never," she says quickly as she wraps her arms around my middle and rests her head against my chest. "Whatever will be, will be. You do what you have to do on that track and let me handle Roscoe."

Holding her close to me, I press my lips against her hair and breathe her in. "I was out of line last night when I hit Roscoe."

"He hit you first. I can't blame you for that."

I should've ducked again and tried to de-escalate the situation instead of hitting him back. The grown-up in me knows that fighting doesn't solve anything, but the other part—the one who's still willing to risk a beatdown to stand my ground—loved getting a lick in. In reality, his face looks worse than mine, which probably drives the dagger deeper into his back and only makes his hatred that much more intense.

"I wish I could've stayed last night. I slept like shit."

"Mom troubles?" She quirks an eyebrow.

"No," I laugh, shaking my head. "I put her on a bus back to Tennessee last night before I came to your place."

"Oh," she says and frowns. "Are you okay? We never got to talk about what happened."

I grip her shoulders, trying to stop myself from kissing her. "I'm fine. She's gone. I want to pretend like she never came to Buxton."

"We'll talk more about her when you're ready and we have

time." She glances over my shoulder at the clock. "I better let you get changed." She stands on her tiptoes and kisses me. "Good luck today, tiger," she whispers against my lips.

"If I beat Roscoe, he'll kill me in my sleep." I laugh and am only partially kidding.

"He's so blind with rage he won't have his mind one hundred percent in this race. If you can beat him, do it."

"What if I beat him? Will you be there when I cross the finish line?"

"I wouldn't dream of being anywhere else." She smiles and touches my face but avoids my bruise.

I kiss her once again. This time deeper, longer, and harder than before. For the next four hours, I need to put my feelings for Faith aside and focus on one thing: kicking Roscoe Ridley's ass.

When Faith leaves, I sit on the bench, staring at my uniform, and wonder if this will be the last time I'll ever wear it.

## FAITH

"Breathe, baby."

My mother squeezes my shoulder tightly as I stare across the track. I gasp, totally unaware I had stopped breathing, or blinking, for that matter. The race is so close between Roscoe and Brooks, I can barely see straight, and I'm worried if I close my eyes, even for a second, I'll miss the most important moment.

They have switched positions at least half a dozen times, and fans are going berserk in the stadium, cheering and hollering for the newest sensation and the man I'm quickly falling in love with. My body tenses as the realization finally hits me.

That's exactly what I've been doing—falling in love with Brooks Carter.

"Fuck," I groan and glance at my mother with wide eyes.

My mother turns to me, her eyebrows drawn down in confusion because she heard that clear as a bell over our headphones. Usually we listen to the pit crew, but today I can't take the stress of overhearing Brooks and Roscoe as they race. Instead, my mother and I tuned into the same channel so we could talk, but we've been so engrossed in the race, we've barely spoken.

I grimace. "Sorry, Mamma."

"You okay?" she asks, waving off my comment.

"I'm fine," I lie. I'm not fine. My heart's pounding so hard, I wonder how much more the muscle can take before finally giving out. "This race is so close."

She nods, leaning forward and up to get a better look. "Let's just hope they don't wreck."

"Mamma!" My eyes widen and my stomach rolls. "You know you can't say stuff like that. It's bad luck."

She pats my leg and smiles. "Don't be silly, child. It's in God's hands now, not some crazy superstition."

I turn my eyes back to the track with a loud huff. Everything's moving so fast as they pass in a blur, I have a hard time finding Brooks's car. But then I spot him. He's on Roscoe's bumper, heading into traffic, about to overtake the racers pulling up the rear. Between the rumble of the engines and the nervous energy coursing through my body, I'm practically vibrating in my seat.

"Two laps to go," Mamma says.

I hold my breath again and rise to my feet, unable to sit down anymore. On the stretch between turns two and three, a bright-orange car comes out of nowhere and takes the lowline as Brooks takes the highline near the wall.

My body stiffens as the guy is fender-to-fender with Brooks as they come out of the turn. "Jesus." I cover my mouth so my mother can't hear as I slur together a string of curse words.

The three cars—Roscoe, the orange bastard, and Brooks—move into a perfect line across the track and head into the final lap neck and neck. They're bumping and grinding, each of them fighting for the lead.

I cover my face and peek through the slits between my fingers. I've never been so stressed out during a race. I bounce on the balls of my feet to stop myself from shaking. Roscoe heads into the final turn, firmly in the lead, but Brooks and the other guy are still duking it out. Brooks takes the outside as he comes out of the turn. He pulls ahead of the orange car but only by a few feet. I'm almost hyperventilating as the flag waves through the air and Roscoe zips underneath it, followed by Brooks and the other guy.

I rip off the headset, letting the roar of the engines hit me at full force. There's nothing like the sexy rumble inside the small stadium. I jump up and down, screaming at the top of my lungs. "He did it! Hell yeah!"

By the time my mother and I walk toward the infield,

the adrenaline starts to wear off and my knees feel like jelly. I didn't realize I'd been tense for the last three hours, practically hanging off the edge of my seat in anticipation.

"I'll be back," I tell my mother before taking off toward Brooks. I push through the celebrating crowd, weaving my way to pit road and wanting nothing more than to congratulate Brooks. "Brooks!" I yell and wave my hands as I run toward his car.

He slides out of the driver's-side window and removes his helmet. His face is smudged with dirt, and the sweat trickling down his cheeks glistens in the sunshine. The man's in his element, looking like pure perfection in his Ridley Racing colors, and I couldn't be prouder. He finally turns, and his eyes meet mine. I run faster, moving toward him like I'm being pulled by some invisible force.

The entire Ridley pit is clear and too busy celebrating with Roscoe to pay much attention to the kid. There aren't too many people around, so I don't even think twice about jumping into Brooks's arms and wrapping my arms around him. "You did it!" I yell, but he can't hear me because I can't even hear myself.

He squeezes me tightly, burying his face against my neck as he spins in a circle. I tip my head back, losing myself in the moment. Brooks's lips graze my neck and bring me right back to reality. I search the grounds, looking for my father or anyone who may have seen us, as Brooks sets my feet back on the ground. I immediately pull away and try to regain my composure. I take a step back and slap him on the shoulder like I'm congratulating a friend. I plaster a smile on my face as my dad comes marching over, hopefully totally unaware of what just happened and still clueless about Brooks and me.

My dad wraps his arm around me and then Brooks, hauling us inward and embracing us both. He's excited, shaking with laughter, and has tears in his eyes. Brooks and I lock eyes, knowing this may be the first and only time we celebrate together, because when my father finds out about us sneaking around, Brooks is going to be sent packing.

# CHAPTER FOURTEEN

## BROOKS

Mr. Ridley pops open another bottle of champagne and holds it high in the air, letting the foam run over his fingers and spill onto the floor. Faith is across the room, in a heated exchange with Roscoe, glancing at me every few seconds before giving him her full attention.

"It's time for a toast," Mr. Ridley says and starts to walk around the room, pouring champagne into the empty glasses of family, friends, and employees who have flowed into Ridley Racing headquarters.

More than fifty people have filled the lobby to celebrate our success, each one of them wearing a Ridley Racing T-shirt with Roscoe's and my names on the back. The excitement is electric, and even though I'd normally not be happy coming in second place, it's hard to be upset when everyone around me is filled with happiness.

A guy like me, barely graduating from high school and with a crappy childhood, should've become a statistic on the evening news. I wasn't supposed to be something or make a name for myself by almost defeating the reigning champion twice in one weekend. But I did. I heard the whispers around town about *the new kid*, but I ignored every single one of them. It's not like I lost to some asshole off the streets. I was beat by the best driver on the entire circuit while the rest of the field choked on our exhaust fumes.

Mr. Ridley stops in front of me, dips his chin, and hands me the half-full champagne bottle. "A glass is not enough for what you did out there today. Hell, the entire weekend, for that matter."

"Thank you, sir." He raises an eyebrow as soon as the word leaves my mouth, and I quickly correct my mistake. "Thanks, Beau."

Mimi touches Beau's arm and hands him another bottle of champagne. He smiles at her like she's the most beautiful person in the world. His eyes light up whenever she walks into a room. I've never seen two people more in love with each other than Beau and Mimi. They have the type of love books are written and movies are created about.

I should be smiling, but I can't. The thought of losing all this—the team, the car, the Ridleys—is more than I can bear. In a short amount of time, I've fallen in love with everything in Buxton, including the people. I've never felt part of anything before. I was always the outsider, the kid no one really wanted to play with, the one parents didn't like because of my mother's nearly daily public antics.

Buxton was my fresh start. A new beginning. Something I could create and mold into what I wanted. And yet...I fucked everything up. I fell for the only girl in town I shouldn't have. What started out as an innocent flirtation and fun turned into something magical and pure. Peering around the room, I soak in the people and excitement, knowing this may be the last time I experience anything quite like this.

Mimi stares down at me, staying behind when Beau walks away. "You doin' okay, kid?"

"I am, ma'am," I lie. I'm the furthest thing from okay. I don't want to say goodbye, and yet, I know that's what is going to happen as soon as Beau finds out I've slept with his daughter and didn't man up and tell him what happened.

She motions toward Faith but keeps her eyes locked on me. "You two okay?"

I drag my gaze across the room, catching sight of Faith among the crowd. My pulse quickens, and I'm momentarily breathless because she's so damn beautiful and good, I don't really deserve her. "We're fine."

"You have to tell my husband what's been going on. You have to tell her father and your boss. It's the only respectable thing to do in your situation," she tells me, but I already know this.

"I was planning to tell him after dinner before my mother showed up, ma'am."

"That's a shame." She touches my shoulder. "Do you love Faith?"

"I do," I say without hesitation.

"Beau's a romantic," she says and turns around for a second, searching for him in the crowd. He's laughing, happy, and I'm going to kill all that as soon as I tell him what happened. "He'll understand. Don't go into too much detail. Just ask for his approval and let him know you love her."

"I wasn't planning on telling him the details." I smirk. I

may be a country bumpkin, but I'm not stupid. Well, that may be debatable since I slept with the boss's daughter, but I'm not going to spill my guts and give him a blow-by-blow retelling of the entire events that led us to this spot. No way. Only someone with a death wish would be that stupid.

"Good. Keep it short and sweet."

I nod and swallow. Short and sweet I can do. The entire confession would probably come flying out of my mouth in a breathless string of words that I'll end up repeating because it'll sound like gibberish. Even now, my body's shaking, knowing I have to man up and do it soon.

"I will. I promise. Thank you, Mimi."

"Don't thank me yet." She laughs and touches my shoulder before she walks away.

Mr. Ridley clears his throat, waiting for the room to grow quiet. I glance at Faith and smile. She waves, but Roscoe pulls her hand down and glares.

The funny thing is...I really like Roscoe. He may have been a pain in the ass, and sometimes he verged on being a whiny little bastard, but he is a champion. I spent two years studying his every move, praying to get a chance to race against him someday.

The room grows quite as Mr. Ridley holds his champagne flute high in the air. "I'm honored to see so many old faces today and a few new ones." He glances in my direction and makes eye contact, and I tip my head to acknowledge his words.

I love and respect Mr. Ridley as a boss and a father. In the six months since he first contacted me, we have formed a quick and easy friendship. That's the thing about him. He is so damn easy to love, with his big bravado and even bigger heart. For a champion and savvy businessman of his caliber, I would've thought he wouldn't be so down-to-earth, but everything about him is filled with kindness and charity.

No one else would have plucked me from the dirt track and laid everything at my feet for the taking. Taking on someone like me is a huge risk for anyone, especially when millions of dollars are at stake, but Mr. Ridley never thought twice about offering me a driver's spot on his team. And how do I repay the man who is giving me biggest opportunity of my life?

*I screw his daughter.*

"Tonight, we're not celebrating just one victory but two. My boys dominated the track."

The room erupts in thunderous applause with people cheering. My vision blurs as tears fill my eyes. God, he always has a way of making me feel like part of the family and not just a driver on his team. Breaking his heart is going to be one of the hardest things I've ever had to do, but I know telling him is right. The truth has to come out, and I only pray he's willing to let me finish the season. I'd do anything to stay on the team. Anything except give up Faith.

"Right now, every competitor hates us. They wish they could be us and replicate our success, but they don't have what I have." He pauses, and his eyes move from Faith to Roscoe to Mimi. "I'm surrounded not only by amazing friends and a loving family. I've been blessed my entire life, and the blessings keep coming with Brooks coming on as the newest addition to the family."

My stomach rolls as guilt washes over me. I am the world's biggest asshole.

"To a long, prosperous, and healthy season. We're about to be unstoppable." He lifts his glass higher, and I raise my champagne bottle, wishing the entire thing was full so I could wash away the sinking feeling that's settling deep in my bones.

## FAITH

I set my purse down on the table and turn toward Brooks, unable to take his silent brooding any longer. "What's wrong?"

He falls backward onto the couch with a loud huff and pulls a fluffy pillow over his face. "Nothing," he mutters as he kicks off his boots, letting them drop to the floor near my coffee table.

I don't waste another second as I cross the room and crawl into his lap. "I can make you feel better." I tangle my fingers in his hair and press my breasts against his chest. He grabs the pillow and tosses it across the room, finally catching sight of my breasts, which are practically spilling out of my top. "Come on, baby. You know you want them." I jiggle my tits in his face when he doesn't say anything.

We haven't touched each other in over a week. There is nothing more I want than to feel his hands and mouth roaming my body and devouring my skin. I want to completely lose myself in him.

Brooks's hands slide up my legs and come to a stop just above my waist. "Princess. I want them more than anything." His fingers dig into my flesh as his grip tightens. His resistance is slipping, and his cock hardens underneath me.

I arch my back and push them closer to his face, trying like hell to get what I want. "You know what I want?" Not above playing dirty, I run my finger down the middle of my cleavage and moan.

His eyes darken as they follow my finger. "What?"

My plan's working, but I know I can't stop now. I have to go bigger, push harder to get him out of whatever funk he's dwelling in. I want the guy who can't keep his hands to himself back, because the Brooks Carter underneath me isn't nearly as fun.

I lean forward, placing my lips next to his ear. "I want you to fuck me in the ass," I whisper with a smile.

His eyes widen. "What?" He swallows and licks his lips, already salivating at the very thought. "You sure? I mean, I'm pretty big. I don't want to hurt you."

I moan and grind against him harder, working the bullshit for everything it's worth. "And my ass is so tight." I'm pulling lines straight out of bad pornos I found in my brother's room as a teenager. I could never figure out why guys like them, because there wasn't anything remotely sexy about the bad cheeseball lines, but clearly the shit works because Brooks is almost panting.

"Fuck," he hisses. "I don't want to hurt you."

This is too easy, but I keep going because it's working like a fucking charm. "Some pain is worth the pleasure, baby." My voice is sugary sweet and filled with need. The need's real, though, until the wanting to have anal sex. There's nothing remotely sexy or pleasurable about booty sex.

He slides his hands to my ass. "You know all the right sexy things to say." He moans and squeezes my ass cheek in the palm of his hand.

Moving my face closer, I stare into his eyes and lower my voice. "My pussy is so full when you're in me, baby. I can't imagine how you'll feel stuffed in my ass."

They say the way to a man's heart is through his stomach, but I'd disagree. The proof is underneath me. Dirty words coupled with the promise of anal sex have gotten me further than a slice of apple pie ever could have.

"Jesus," he murmurs against my lips before sealing his mouth over mine.

My skin tingles as his rough palm slides across my back, and I rock against him. He moves his thumbs underneath the elastic of my bra, and in one quick motion, he unhooks my bra like he's done it a thousand times.

Breaking the kiss, I lift my arms over my head, wanting nothing more than to get naked with this man. He pulls his shirt off and drops it to the floor. I keep my eyes locked on his as my hands slide down his rock-hard chest.

"God, you're beautiful," he whispers as he gazes up at me.

He slides the pads of his thumbs across the tender undersides of my breasts, and my nipples instantly harden. I'm hungry for his kiss, starving for his cock, and practically panting with need for any little bit of him he'll give. He moves his hands upward, enveloping my breasts, and I tip my head back, offering myself to him as I dig my fingernails into his shoulder. "Shh, princess. I know exactly what you need."

I'm so lost in his touch, so consumed by the feel of his coarse palms against my nipples, I can't protest. He leans forward, pressing his lips to my neck, and nips the tender skin near my shoulder, which he knows drives me insane. I lie helpless in his arms with my eyes closed, unable to speak as his lips burn my skin and leave goose bumps in their wake.

When his hands leave my breasts, I whimper and open my eyes, longing for his warmth and silently begging for his touch. He hooks an arm around my waist and lifts me into the air, setting my feet flat on the floor. I sway slightly, my head swimming with possibilities as he works the button and zipper of my jeans and yanks them down my legs. As I step out of them, I admire him from this position as he lifts his ass and pulls his jeans off. His muscles glisten in the light, rippling one-by-one as he moves. The planes of his abs deepen as he twists, creating caverns of skin I could lose myself in.

He motions to me with his hand and beckons me forward. "Come here."

I move quickly, mounting him again and take in his rugged beauty beneath me. "Do you want me, Brooks?" My lower half rocks against him, his cock sliding easily through my wetness.

He wraps an arm around my back and leans forward, bringing his lips near mine as he stares up at me. "More than anything." His voice is ragged, matching his hard breaths.

Whatever happened before tonight doesn't matter. The only thing I can focus on is the feel of his dick skating across my clit, sending me closer to the edge. I close my eyes, rocking back and forth, back and forth, relishing the warm, wet skin-on-skin sensation.

His face comes forward, and he wraps his lips around my nipple, adding to the building pressure and deepening my need. I moan softly and push my pussy against him harder as he toys with the hard tip between his teeth.

"More," I beg, needing more than the friction as our bodies move together.

He lifts me and pulls his lips away from my breast. I cry out but am quickly silenced as he drags the tip of his cock between my legs. "You want this cock, princess?"

"Yes," I moan, breathless and so horny I'm ready to spear myself on his length because I've never enjoyed being teased. Especially when I'm naked and so turned on my entire body is shaking.

The slickened tip presses against my opening as he slowly pushes the hardness inside me, filling me inch-by-inch and entirely too slow. I ease myself down and try to make him go faster, but he stares up at me, grinning and enjoying every moment of the delicious torture.

Unable to take it a moment longer, I spread my knees and bury them in the cushions of the couch, forcing his dick deeper.

"You don't play fair." He smirks as he slides his hand up my back to my neck and tangles his fingers in my hair. I gaze at him as he tips my head a little to the side, holding my face near his. "You and that greedy pussy will be the death of me."

My insides clench around his steel shaft because I love when he talks dirty to me. "Shut up and fuck me." I pull my body up before slamming myself back down as my hair remains firmly in his grasp.

His lips part and his eyes are locked on mine as I ride his length. He growls and digs his fingertips into my hip to control the movement and speed as we fuck. "Slower."

The moment is intense and intimate. I slowly rock forward, my eyes still on his, locked in an embrace. He pulls my mouth toward his and seals his lips around mine, stealing my moans and deepening our connection.

I melt into him, completely lost in his hands, his mouth, his everything. Our tongues dance around each other as he holds my body to his, and I ride his cock at a torturously slow pace. His hand falls away from my hair and skates over my back before cupping my ass, grinding me harder against him. My clit throbs with each stroke of his body against it, and my body shudders as the climax I so badly need stays just out of reach.

I tense momentarily as his hand drifts between my legs and his fingers slide through my wetness and against my opening. I'm already stuffed to the max with his cock and can't imagine another inch inside me.

"Baby, relax," he murmurs against my lips as he pulls his fingers backward to linger near my asshole. "I'll make you feel good."

I manage to get his name past my lips before he crashes his mouth down and a single digit rubs the outside of the one place I said he could have tonight. The sensation is so intense that every muscle in my body shudders uncontrollably. I gasp against his lips and can almost feel him smile.

Circling the outside with more pressure, he spreads the wetness across the delicate and sensitive skin.

Jesus. No one has ever touched me there, and the sensation isn't what I expect. My lower half moves faster as his finger presses against my asshole, sending a lightning bolt throughout my body. "Yes," I moan and squeeze his cock with every muscle inside my pussy as I drive his shaft deeper.

Brooks pulls his head away and stares up at me as he slides the tip of his finger through my forbidden tightness. I freeze, so overcome with the full feeling of his finger and cock.

"My dirty girl likes her ass touched." He smirks, and I gasp when he pushes his finger deeper, sending me right over the edge.

My body quakes, and I'm now incapable of keeping our smooth, steady rhythm as pleasure rushes through every inch of my body. Taking over, he lifts his hips and impales me with his cock while his finger is buried so far in my ass that I'm unable to breathe.

Moments later, both of our bodies are trembling, covered in sweat, as we tumble together in an earth-shattering orgasm. No sound fills the room except for our labored breathing, and the smell of sex surrounds us as we gasp for air.

# CHAPTER FIFTEEN

## BROOKS

I'm at Ridley Racing thirty minutes before everyone else, except for Mr. Ridley. With the offices empty, the place is eerily quiet, and I can almost hear my heart pounding in my chest. I run through my speech as I approach his door, pausing a few feet away to take a deep breath. I know this is a make or break moment, and one wrong word could have my ass packing and on my way.

"Beau." I knock on his office door and shake out my hands, trying to get my fear under control. The one thing I know about Mr. Ridley is that he appreciates honesty, which I have kind of already fucked up.

"Come in."

I hold my breath and push open the door. This is it. The moment I'd been dreading but knew was coming. The only thing I could do now is be honest. If necessary, I'd throw myself at his feet and beg for forgiveness, but not until all other options had been exhausted.

He glances up from a pile of paperwork. He smiles as soon as he sees me, and I hate that what I'm about to say will wipe away his happiness. "You're here early, Brooks."

I walk in with my head held high, even though I'm a wreck inside. "May I have a moment of your time? There's something I need to talk to you about."

He motions to the chair across from his desk before he leans back in his. "Sit."

"I'd rather stand if you don't mind." I grip the back of the chair, grounding myself and keeping my knees from giving out. Any other man on the planet wouldn't send me into a panic the way Beau Ridley does. It's not because he's my boss or Faith's father, but I grew up idolizing the guy and wishing I was his kid. Now I'm here and part of his team, ready and willing to fuck everything up in a heartbeat.

"I wanted to talk to you anyway. Sit down. No important conversation should be had unless both parties are eye to eye."

*Jesus.* I slowly lower myself into the chair, feeling like I've been called into the principal's office for a stern lecture about my unacceptable behavior. Whatever pressing matter he needs to talk to me about pales in comparison to the news I'm about to throw in his lap. I'm sure once I come clean, I won't need to stick around for whatever else he has on his mind.

I rub my hands together with my elbows resting on my knees and lower my head. "I need to talk to you first before we go any further."

"Go ahead."

I'm totally gutted and ready to throw up, but I man up and start the prepared speech I'd practiced twenty times on the way over here. "So." I pause as the words stick in my throat. I take a deep breath and decide I just have to spill and talk fast. "I've fallen in love with your daughter, sir. I tried not to. I tried to ignore her, but no matter what I did, I couldn't stay away. I've never felt..."

"Stop."

I place my hands on my knees, bringing my eyes to his, and brace myself for whatever he's about to say.

"Say that slower." He crosses his arms over his chest and stills.

"Which part?" I swallow.

"All of it."

"I'm in love with your daughter, sir." I blink and pause as he stares at me with an unreadable face. My eyes widen as I wait for him to lunge across the desk and grab me by the throat, but he doesn't.

We sit in awkward silence. Every second that ticks by seems like an hour. My nervousness intensifies as my leg begins to bounce uncontrollably. There is no smile on his face. He hasn't moved an inch since I've repeated the most important part of my speech. I don't know if I should say something more or just keep staring at him while he processes the information.

I'm about to open my mouth when he says, "Did you tell her?"

*Wait. What?* "Um," I mumble and rub my hands against my jeans. "She knows."

He leans forward and rests his hands on his desk, clasping them together. "Have you *told* her?"

"Well. I..." I pause and blow out a shaky breath. "Yes, sir."

"I may not be the smartest hog in the pen, but I know when something is happening on my farm."

"I never thought you were stupid, sir," I say quickly, ready to throw myself at him and beg for forgiveness.

"I have eyes, and my wife can't keep a secret worth a damn neither. Faith is a grown woman, and I can't tell her what to do in life, even though I want to."

"So, you're okay with us?"

He takes a deep breath but doesn't seem to relax. "I wasn't okay with you two sneaking behind my back and the fact that you didn't come to me man to man."

I hang my head, regretting not being more up front, but damn, I never expected to fall in love with his daughter. "I didn't want to disappoint you."

"Listen, son. I don't have a problem with you dating my daughter. I understand what it's like to be crazy in love with someone and worry about getting approval from her father. Hell"—he laughs—"Mimi's father hated me. He told her I'd never amount to much more than a grease monkey and that I was beneath her social class. It did not matter what that old bastard said. I was going to marry Mimi whether he liked it or not. Love is not something we can control or contain. The first time I saw Mimi, I knew she'd be my wife. I couldn't imagine a single day without setting eyes on her beautiful face and hearing her voice."

I nod, knowing exactly what he's saying. "I understand how that feels."

"Just do right by her. If you love her, tell her. If you can't imagine life without her in it, make her yours and don't for a second make Faith regret a moment of loving you."

"I can do that, sir." I smile.

"'Cause if you break her heart, I'll bust your legs."

I grimace. I have no doubt he'll do worse than that. "You're not going to say she's too good for someone like me?"

He waves his hand. "Don't be ridiculous. When I look at you, I see a champion in the making. Who you were before you stepped foot in Buxton is none of my business and has no bearing on what transpires going forward. I know what happened between you and Roscoe." He touches his cheek.

"He's upset about Faith and me."

"He's upset at the world, kid. Don't take it personally. He'll come around. Just give him time. Letting him win yesterday was a step in the right direction, though, but don't do it again. If you can win, do it. Roscoe needs to eat a slice of humble pie every once in a while."

"Um," I mumble because I thought I was pretty slick. I could've won yesterday. There were more than a few spots I could've taken the lead but didn't. I thought it was best if I let Ridley win the first race in front of his hometown crowd. If I did not, his hatred and resentment toward me would only grow and eventually spiral into a mess that would have me on the losing end.

"Again, ain't dumb, son."

"Sorry," I apologize again. "Thank you, Beau."

"Now get out of here. I have work to do before we head out on the road tomorrow for Bristol. Dinner tonight at seven."

"I'll be there, Beau." I stand and start toward the door, relief washing over me with every step.

"And Brooks."

I pause and turn.

"Show her how you feel and never stop."

## FAITH

The coffee shop near my place is more crowded than usual. I finally dragged myself out of bed after sleeping right through my alarm. Brooks kept me up half the night, but I can't complain. I may feel like a member of the walking dead, but my muscles ache in the most delicious way.

"Medium or large today, Faith?" asks Anna May, the local coffee goddess and my old high school friend, likely sensing what I'm going to order.

I stare at her with glassy eyes and force a smile on my face. "As big as ya got, honey, and an extra shot."

"Late night?" she asks as she takes the credit card from my hand.

"Something like that."

She twists her lips together and leans over the counter, moving closer as she hands back my card. "Good for you," she whispers with a wink.

I step to the side of the counter as I wait, scrolling through my favorite app so I don't have to engage in small talk anymore. We're only a weekend into the season, and I'm already exhausted. The town gossip surrounding Brooks and Constance has finally died down, but I know once Brooks and I come out, the news will spread like wildfire. The only saving grace is that by the time that happens, we'll be on our way to Bristol.

"Here you go, Faith," Anna May says as she places the to-go cup on the counter. "You ain't lookin' so good, honey."

I grab the cup and bring it to my nose, inhaling the

heavenly scent. "I'm just tired, Anna May. You know how it is."

She's her usual energetic self—probably self-medicated with enough caffeine to keep an elephant awake. I know if I worked here, I'd down cappuccinos like water and probably buzz across the floor instead of walk. "The season just started. You better get your ass in gear and start taking some vitamins, or you're going to wear yourself out."

I laugh, wishing it were that easy to get through the very long and hot racing season ahead.

"I saw you hug that boy yesterday. He have anything to do with those bags under your eyes?" She gives me a sappy grin.

*Oh shit.* I didn't think anyone saw us, but I should've known better. Every person in Buxton was at the track yesterday, and it was foolish of me to think everyone had their eyes on Roscoe. "No. Just been busy with work." The last thing I want is for my business with Brooks Carter to become the talk of the town. "I better run before I'm late."

"Stop in sometime when you're not in such a rush and have a cup with me."

"Yeah, May. I'll do that," I lie through my teeth. She's not only the best barista south of the Mason-Dixon line, she's also a gossip.

I step outside and lean against the building, letting the sun warm my face. As I take a sip, Roscoe jogs across the street, waving his hand like I have energy enough to walk away.

"Got a minute?" he asks.

I hold up a finger, taking another sip before I answer. "What's up? If you're going to lecture me some more, you can save your breath."

"I'm your brother." He says those words like they're carte blanche for being an asshole whenever he feels like it. I've never once lectured him for his shitty choices, not even when I found out he was dipping his wick in the Constance ugly well.

"You have one minute."

"Someone's grumpy today," he teases with a smile, but I'm in no mood, and he knows it. "Okay. I thought long and hard about what happened."

"Hmm," I mumble against the rim of my coffee cup, electing to take another sip instead of speaking.

He rubs the back of his neck and glances toward the ground. "I was wrong."

My entire body rocks backward, and I turn my ear toward him, figuring I had to hear him wrong. My brother never admits being wrong about anything. Not even the smallest, least trivial shit in the world. He'd rather go down in flames than admit to being wrong about anything. "Say that again?"

He laughs. "I was wrong about getting involved with you and Brooks." He rubs his hands together and blows out a breath. "It wasn't my place. I never should've hit him. I just felt..."

"I get it," I say, giving him an out and a relief from the guilt that's probably been eating at him. After the race, I laid everything out for him. I told him I loved Brooks, and he needed to learn to accept it.

"It's just all so quick. I'm worried he's going to break your heart."

"There's never a guarantee when it comes to love, Roscoe. Whether I'm with him for a week or twenty years, there's always a chance of being hurt. But I'm sick of denying there's something growing between us. I can't describe it, but it's real. I've never been drawn to someone the way I am to him. When we..."

"Stop." He places his hand in the air and shows me his palm. "I don't want to know."

I laugh and bat his hand away. "Don't be an idiot."

"I've never experienced anything like that, Faith."

"You've never been in love," I tell him. A few weeks ago, I would've laughed in someone's face if they told me they believed in love at first sight. But now, after what I've been through, I can say it's one hundred percent real.

"You're my sister, and I'll always worry about you."

"You can worry, but I'm a big girl, Roscoe. I don't need you fighting my battles for me anymore. I'm not that shy little girl, needing rescuing by her big brother."

"Whether you need rescuing or not, I'll always have your back because I love you."

I lean forward, popping up on my toes, and kiss my big brother's cheek. "I love you too."

"Want to ride to the office with me?"

I know better than to say yes. I was barely awake, but I didn't need to have a near-death experience before eight. "Um, no. I'll take my own car because I like my life."

"Suit yourself, kid. Are we okay?"

"We're fine," I reassure him. I can let things go. What happened at my apartment between him and Brooks was in the past. I couldn't fault him for lashing out after being caught off guard. "Just learn to use your words instead of your fists from now on. Okay?"

"I can do words," he tells me. "I'm a master at wording."

I roll my eyes and shoo him away. I hope Brooks is having an easier time with my father than he did with my brother, but knowing my daddy, he's keeping his hands to himself.

# CHAPTER SIXTEEN

## BROOKS

"This doesn't look good," Faith says as we pull into her parents' driveway just before seven.

Beau's waiting on the front steps with Roscoe by his side, their arms crossed in front of their chests, staring at us as I park the car.

"I thought you said everything went well today."

I put the car in park and watch them through the windshield, worried that maybe something changed in the last few hours. "It did. Shit. I thought we ended with an understanding."

She motions toward them and shakes her head. "Whatever it is, this is not good."

"Not good" may be the understatement of the year.

Faith climbs out of the truck and makes her way to her father as I follow behind, eyeing Roscoe. "Hey, Daddy. What's wrong?"

"Nothing, pumpkin." He cradles her face in his hands and kisses her cheek softly. "Can you go inside and help your mother while we have a moment?"

*Oh shit.* Nothing about the statement along with the way

they're looking at me says I'm in for anything good.

Faith peers over her shoulder, and I nod. "Okay. Don't be out here too long," she says, dragging her gaze between her father and brother.

"Everything's fine, sweetheart. Go inside," her father tells her.

They stare at me as I stand on the driveway and wait for Faith to walk inside and close the door. When the door finally closes, Mr. Ridley peers at the window to make sure Faith has walked far enough away. "It's your mother."

I rub my forehead and groan. I thought she'd leave after I made it very clear I want nothing more to do with her and threw some money her way to get out of town. I should've known better.

"She went to a local reporter and spilled your life story," Roscoe blurts out.

"What?" I clench my teeth. My heart's beating so wildly out of control my eardrums pound and become deafening. I squeeze my eyes shut and see the color red.

Mr. Ridley steps forward and places his hand on my shoulder. "We'll be on the road for the next few weeks, but she can easily find us. It's best if we take care of this as soon as possible. I'll get the PR team on the story immediately and make sure we release an official statement."

"I'll do whatever you need and want. What about the reporter?"

"He's an old friend, so don't worry. He'll never print her trash, but I'm not sure who else she'll try to sell her lies to. I'll find out, and we'll make sure the truth comes out."

I breathe a sigh of relief at the saving grace of small-town life. Anywhere else, and her convoluted story would be printed in tomorrow's paper instead of landing in the trash basket.

"Now, boys. Put a smile on your face and enjoy dinner. If we don't, there'll be hell to pay from the ladies inside this house. Understood?"

"Yes," Roscoe and I say at the same time.

Mr. Ridley enters the house first, followed by Roscoe and then myself. I'm glad he thinks this conversation is going to be easy to gloss over, but knowing Faith, she's not going to let it go.

We are barely able to move with so much food in our bellies. Mrs. Ridley cooked a feast that could've fed a small army instead of five people, but I will not complain. Home-cooked meals are something I never had but could get used to. Somehow, though, I don't see Faith as the domestic goddess her mother is.

Faith rests her head on my shoulder as we sit on the couch. She keeps her hands in her lap, and I keep mine at my side because we're in her parents' home and I would like to get out of here alive.

"What was that about when we first got here?" she whispers in my ear.

"Just business." I glance at Roscoe and Beau, but they are too busy watching television and in a food coma to even hear us.

She moves her hand to my knee and squeezes it tightly. "Don't lie to me."

"I made everyone's favorite," Mrs. Ridley announces and walks into the living room holding the biggest carrot cake I have ever seen.

At this rate, with Mrs. Ridley overfeeding us, I will not be able to fit in my suit next weekend. I keep eating everything she puts in front of me and can't seem to tell her no. It is a problem I have with both women in this family and something I don't think will ever change.

"Mamma, you're going to have to roll me out of here," Roscoe says.

"Everyone has to have at least a bite. I spent hours making this."

"We'll all take a slice, my darling," Mr. Ridley tells her, answering for all of us to make his wife happy.

She smiles at him as she places the tower of sugar on the coffee table in front of us. "I'll get the plates."

When she walks out of the room, Faith squeezes my leg again but harder. "I'm not going to ask again. What did my dad and Roscoe want?"

I peer down at her before kissing her forehead. "We'll talk about it later," I say softly and try to satisfy her enough to stop her interrogation and not break my word to her father.

"You will tell me."

I smile and laugh softly. "I tell you everything."

"You will."

I have no doubt she speaks the truth. Faith has a way of getting me to talk, even when I don't want to. I have seen Mrs. Ridley skillfully extract information from her husband, and Faith learned by watching her mother handle her father like a pro. There is no use in fighting, because I know Faith won't stop until she gets exactly what she wants.

## FAITH

I grip the sheets in my hands as my knuckles turn white, and my knees start to buckle. "Harder!"

"You want it deeper?" He rears back, taking his cock with him before slamming back into me with so much force I rock forward on my tiptoes to stay upright.

I push my ass backward, meeting each of his thrusts. He places his mouth next to my ear and grabs my hair in the palm of his hands. "Maybe you want it in your ass," he whispers.

"Brooks!" Roscoe pounds on the door.

I stop breathing and peer over my shoulder at Brooks. His eyes are wide, matching my own, as we both turn toward the door with our lower bodies motionless. I'm so close to orgasm, I can barely see straight, and every muscle in my body aches in the most delicious way because of Brooks.

"What the hell?" I groan into the mattress as Brooks scoops his jeans off the floor and heads for the door, mumbling something under his breath about Roscoe being an asshole.

He bounces up and down, trying to pull his tight and super-sexy jeans on and having difficulty because of his erection.

"Brooks! Open the goddamn door!"

"Coming. Jesus," Brooks mutters as he tries to zip up his jeans. Giving up, he opens the door to find Roscoe with his hands on either side of the doorframe, breathing heavily and soaking wet. "What the fuck, man?"

"What's wrong?" I wrap my arms around his middle and

peer around his shoulder at my brother. “We were sleeping.”

His eyes dart to mine before returning to Brooks. “It’s your place.”

“My trailer?”

“Yeah. It’s destroyed.”

I gasp and cover my mouth. *Destroyed?* It is not like the thing was a palace, but losing everything without any warning is more than one person should have to bear. Especially someone like Brooks, with so few things to his name as it is.

Brooks jerks backward, taking me with him. “How?”

“Your mother was found at the scene with a bottle of vodka and a lighter.”

Brooks scrubs his hand down his face and sighs. “Is she in custody?”

“Yeah.”

“Good,” I say.

Roscoe gawks at Brooks. “That’s all you got to say? All your stuff is gone.”

“Roscoe, I learned a long time ago that things don’t matter. I’ll buy new shirts. I’ll find new jeans. As long as Faith’s safe and my mom gets help, I’m happy.”

“Dude,” Roscoe groans. “I’d be flipping my shit right now.”

“Everything I need is right here, man. I came from nothing, and I know how to survive without stuff.”

“I’m so sorry.” I tighten my hold on him and place my cheek against his back. “It’s all because of me.”

He turns, lifting my face upward as I keep my arms wrapped around him. “This has nothing to do with you, princess. She’s crazy. All that matters is that we’re both safe.”

"I'm glad you stayed over tonight. I can't imagine if..." My voice trails off as the nightmare scenario plays in my head.

Brooks could've very easily been inside when she decided to have a hillbilly bonfire. The very thought makes my blood turn cold and leaves me breathless.

"Don't think it." He presses his lips against my mouth and swallows my whimper. "Everything will be okay."

Roscoe clears his throat and waits as we have a moment. Standing there, staying silent, can't be easy for him. I know he wants to probably punch Brooks in the face again, but somehow, he remains civil as we both turn to face him. "We're pulling out in five hours. I'll have a new trailer prepped for you while we're on the road and will have it ready to go. So, don't worry about where you're going to stay."

"Don't go to all that trouble, man."

"You have to stay somewhere."

I take a step forward and place my hand on Brooks's chest. "He's staying with me in my trailer, Roscoe."

Brooks's eyes widen in shock. "I am?"

Roscoe hangs his head and grumbles under his breath, but he keeps his unhappiness to himself. "Whatever you want."

"I have plenty of room, and that trailer wouldn't be road ready in time."

"Fine. Fine." Roscoe pushes off the doorframe and straightens. "I thought you should know what happened and that you two were safe tonight."

"Thanks for letting us know," Brooks replies with his arm around my shoulder.

"Night, Roscoe," I say as he jogs down the narrow stairwell

to the door leading outside.

Brooks scoops me into his arms and carries me toward the bed. "We need to talk, princess." Those are the words no one ever wants to hear. He sits on the edge and holds me in his arms. He gazes at me, sweeping a strand of hair away from my face with the back of his fingers.

"What's wrong?" I stare into his eyes as the butterflies start to flutter inside me.

He kisses me softly with his hand cupping my face and his thumb gently brushing against my cheek. He pulls away a moment later and rests his forehead against mine. "I love you, Faith. I've never loved another person more than I love you." His hold tightens, and he closes his eyes. "The thought of losing you terrifies me."

The butterflies inside my stomach start to buzz around, almost knocking into each other. Tears form in my eyes as I stare at him, knowing that it couldn't have been easy for him to confess his feelings after how he'd grown up. "I love you too, Brooks."

"Promise me you'll never put yourself in jeopardy."

"I promise."

"Promise me you'll always come to me if you're worried."

"I promise."

"Promise me you'll marry me."

"I promise."

My eyes widen as the realization of what he asked and what I agreed to finally hits me.

"What?" I whisper so quietly I can barely hear myself speak.

"I want nothing more than for you to be mine." He lifts me in the air and places me on the bed before kneeling in front of me. "Faith Ridley, will you marry me and be mine forever?"

Covering my mouth with my hands, I let out an ear-shattering screech as he opens a box with the most beautiful diamond inside. I'm so overcome and in such total shock I can barely breathe, let alone speak. Sticking my hand out and wiggling my fingers, I nod frantically as my eyes fill with tears.

"Is that a yes?" He pulls the tiny princess cut diamond out and drops the box to the floor.

"Yes!" I'm so happy I do not even let him slip the ring on my finger. I leap into his arms and start to pepper his face with kisses.

He laughs and falls backward from the impact, but I don't let that stop me. I straddle his sides and finally make my way to his lips. "I love you," I say because I want to hear him say the words back to me again.

"I love you too, princess."

People are going to think we are mad—well, everyone except my parents. They eloped after knowing each other for only three weeks. They knew they were meant to be, just like I know Brooks Carter is meant to be mine forever.

# EPILOGUE

## BROOKS

She's been in the bathroom for over a half hour. I pace outside the bathroom, dressed and ready to roll because we're already late. "Faith. Come on."

"One more minute," she says.

"What's wrong?"

"Nothing."

She's lying. There's a loud crash from inside the bathroom, followed by a few curse words. I push open the door and find her sitting on the linoleum surrounded by a half dozen tiny white sticks.

"What the hell?"

"Fuck," she groans and stares up at the sky light.

I step inside and take a closer look at the mess. My body rocks backward as I realize what's lying near her feet. "Are you?"

Her eyes narrow as she focuses her gaze on me. "You knocked me up."

"How?" The wind is knocked out of me as I stand there in shock, staring at her and the six positive pregnancy tests.

She grabs a stick and holds it in the air, jiggling it as she does. "You had sex with me. Duh!"

I'm going to be a father? *What?*

I never thought I'd have children of my own. Never in a million years did I ever imagine having a wife, let alone a family. The doctor had told me it would be almost impossible after the injury I sustained, but clearly, he was wrong.

I drop to my knees and pull her into my arms. "We'll be okay."

I'm not sure if I'm trying to reassure her or myself. I do not know the first thing about raising kids. With a crappy mother and a missing dad, I feel totally helpless and clueless.

She clutches my T-shirt and presses her face into my chest. "Oh, God. I'm going to have stretch marks and a big ass."

I hold her tighter. "I'll love every inch of that ass, princess."

"None of my clothes are going to fit, and my breasts are going to be so big they'll likely slap me in the face when I go for a jog."

"For real. You're selling me on this pregnancy thing. Giant tits. What else can a man ask for?" I laugh and kiss the top of her head.

Part of me is joking, but the other part is already imagining her belly with my baby inside and her curvy body, riding on top of me. The image is sexier than I ever imagined.

She slaps my chest and peers up at me. "This is serious, Brooks. We're going to be responsible for another human."

"You're going to be a wonderful mother."

"I'm scared."

Scared doesn't even begin to describe how I feel as the news settles and becomes reality. I'm petrified and worried

I'm going to mess up some little helpless soul as much as my parents did me.

"How do you think I feel? I don't know the first thing about raising kids."

She touches my face and smiles at me tenderly. "You know what not to do, and you're one of the most loving and protective people I know. You're going to be a wonderful daddy."

I love the sound of that word.

*Daddy.*

"I thought you were on the pill."

She glares at me. "The day after we got drunk and had sex, I couldn't remember if I took my pill the day before. So..."

"So, this wasn't my fault." I raise an eyebrow.

Her eyes widen. "Are you saying it's mine?"

"Baby," I say and pull her tighter. "It's no one's fault. It's a freaking miracle and blessing."

"Now we have to tell my father."

I thought breaking the news to Mr. Ridley about dating his daughter was difficult, but having him find out that I knocked her up—and out of wedlock no less—is going to be damn near frightening.

## FAITH

Stepping inside my father's trailer and about to break some life-changing news may very well be the scariest thing I've ever had to do. He's always been so proud of me, bragging to all his friends about the "good girl" Faith he raised the right way. My heart breaks a little knowing my dad is never going to be able to look at me the same way.

"Wait here," I say to Brooks as I release his hand and walk toward my father. Country music blares in the distance from the party tent outside Bristol, and people are everywhere, drunk and happy.

He steps forward, following me, but I stop him. "I should be there," he pleads.

"I need to do this."

He nods, and I slowly approach my father as he sits at the dining room table, sipping on a beer. "Hey, Daddy. Where's Mamma?"

"She's in the bathroom getting ready. What's wrong, pumpkin?" He pats the seat next to him and glances at Brooks, who hasn't moved from the doorway.

"Don't freak out." I smile nervously and set my hand on my stomach almost out of instinct.

My father's eyes dart to Brooks and narrow. "Someone better say something before I jump to the wrong conclusion."

I slide into the chair and grab his hand, clutching it in mine. "I wanted to talk to you first about something very important."

"Are you sick?" His eyes search my face, but I smile and try to calm his fears.

"No, Daddy. It's nothing like that."

"Jane?"

"No. She's still in jail."

He adjusts his body in the chair and moves closer to me. "What is it, then?"

He's already jumped to the worst possible scenarios to begin with, so hopefully the news about me being with child won't sting quite as much.

"I'm pregnant," I say quickly, spilling the beans because I've already tortured him enough.

He stares at me with an unreadable look before his eyes drift to Brooks. He's silent, and I can't tell if he's about to catapult himself across the room and wrap his fingers around Brooks's neck or so overcome with joy he can't form words.

"How?" he asks, but I don't answer—discussing sex with my father has always been awkward. "I know how, but..."

"Yeah."

"When? Wait, I don't want to know that either." He covers his mouth with one hand while squeezing my hand with the other. "You sure, pumpkin?"

"Six tests say I am, Daddy."

He practically jumps out of his seat and whoops, holding his head in disbelief. "Mimi, get your ass out here, darling. We have something to celebrate."

"I'm almost done," Mamma says from inside the bathroom.

"You're not mad?" I haven't moved. I'm still in shock because I expected my dad to lose his mind when he found out that not only were we sneaking behind his back, but I had been careless enough to get knocked up.

He stops and leans forward, cupping my chin in his hands. "Baby girl. You're a woman, and how could I ever be mad that you're going to give me my first grandbaby?"

"But we're not married."

He shakes his head and laughs. "Neither were your mamma and me when we conceived Roscoe."

"I know, Daddy."

"Your mamma and I are old-school. It was a big no-no to have sex before marriage back then. Today things are different."

I blink and stare at my father. Who is this man before me, and where's my daddy?

"Brooks," he says and storms toward Brooks.

Just like me, Brooks expects my father to lose his shit at any second, and he starts to back up. "I'm sorry, sir."

"Don't be silly." My father wraps his arms around Brooks and lifts him into the air. "We're having a baby."

Brooks stares at me over my father's shoulder, helpless in his arms as my father gives him a bear hug. "We are."

When my father finally places Brooks back on the ground, he grabs him by the shoulder and leans forward. "Now listen, son."

"Yes, sir," Brooks replies and takes a deep breath.

"No more sir or Beau. You can call me Dad from now on. Ya hear?"

My nose twitches, and tears fill my eyes as I stare at them from across the room.

"Yes," Brooks says and pauses, sounding like he's choked up too. "Dad."

My father knows exactly what he's doing. He knows every bit about Brooks's past because he did an extensive background check before letting him step foot in Buxton. None of it matters to my father.

"What's all the commotion out here?" Mamma says as she steps foot out of the bathroom in a pair of dark blue jeans, cowboy boots, and a white blouse. "I thought we weren't going dancing for another half hour."

My father practically floats across the floor and sweeps my mother off her feet. "You ready to get down, Grandma?"

"What?" She tenses in his arms, and her head practically snaps in my direction. "You're pregnant?"

"Yeah," I say with a forced smile because she may not be as overjoyed as my father.

"We're going to be grandparents?" she asks my father because she doesn't quite believe it.

Brooks comes to my side and rests his hand on my shoulder. I place my hand over his and stare at my parents. My father holds my mother like she's the most precious thing in the world. With parents like them, I have no doubt we'll raise our baby with so much love, they'll want for nothing.

I glance up and smile at Brooks. *I love you,* I mouth.

"I love you too," he replies and gets down on one knee. I tangle my fingers in his hair as he places his hands on my stomach and leans forward. "I love you too, baby. I haven't even met you yet, but I already know you've stolen my heart. I'm going to be the best daddy anyone's ever had." Brooks glances up at me with a smile that touches his cheeks and tears in his eyes, matching mine. "I'm finally going to have something I never had... A family of my own."

ALSO AVAILABLE FROM
WATERHOUSE PRESS

***Keep reading for an excerpt!***

# EXCERPT FROM
## MISADVENTURES WITH A MANNY

I run my hand through my hair and inhale and exhale deeply before my next sip of wine. I haven't left the island since my fight with Charlie. Looking at the computer screen, I search through each of the nannies on the site. None of them are qualified enough for my kids. They're either too young and not able to drive or too old and would probably die of a heart attack when my kids do whatever they are gonna do to them. I need someone strong, someone able to handle three rough, tough, hurting boys.

God, I hate that they are hurting.

Leaning back in my chair, I shut my computer and shake my head. I'm going to have to take the day off tomorrow. My boss, Richard, will not appreciate that, but what else can I do?

*Damn it.*

Just before I dial his number, I hear my name.

"Vera."

It's Riana.

I almost cry out in joy. I didn't want to ask her to come; she's done enough. But being the great sister she is, she is here. I stand up, throw back the rest of my wine, and put my glass in the sink. "I'm in the kitchen."

I hear the sounds of the boys running down the stairs and then their chatter as Riana scolds them. "Really? Duct tape?"

"She was awful," Charlie says simply.

"She didn't like loud noises," Elliot adds.

"And we're loud," Louis says.

The trill of her laughter mixed with Phillip's runs down my spine as I head toward the living room. I don't want them to feed into the boys' madness, but that's their right as their aunt and uncle, I guess. Turning the corner, I try to smile, but I'm caught off guard when a pair of light-gray eyes meet mine.

And they do not belong to my sister or brother-in-law.

Holy. Shit. Who the hell is this?

I'm stunned and blinking as I take in the man. I always thought Phillip was tall, but this guy towers over him. His shoulders are broad but not too broad—the perfect size. His waist is trim and his legs so darn long. His dark hair is a mess at the top but nicely shaved up the sides. He wears a simple pair of jeans with a button-down flannel that looks tight at his shoulders. I have never been attracted to someone who wears flannel. Simon normally wore suits, or dress shirts with pressed jeans, yet I am drooling over this guy in flannel.

But that isn't what has my gut in knots. No. It's his eyes—such a light gray, they remind me of beautiful storm clouds. I feel lost in them as we look at each other. Blinking, I take in the sweet freckles on his face, which remind me of Elliot's. Those freckles are the only thing that helps me tell the boys apart, but on this man, they aren't adorable; they are sexy. And holy shit, he has a beard. It's nicely trimmed, giving him a distinguished look.

A fucking sexy look.

*Jesus.*

It's hard to tear my gaze from his. He's drinking me in. I feel his stare burn all over my skin. As he turns his gaze down my face to my neck, he stops. What the hell? Following where his eyes are aimed, I realize I have a few too many buttons undone. Heat explodes along my chest as I hurriedly fasten up my blouse so there is a lot less of me exposed. Looking up to see if anyone notices, I see him watching me, those light eyes wanting more.

Who the hell is this guy?

And why am I hot?

I look to my sister, my eyes wide. She looks back at me, and I don't miss the little grin that pulls at her lips.

"I am here to rescue all of you." The man smiles.

"Hey! Linc! What's up?" says Charlie.

He holds out his hand to shake Charlie's.

"Been on the field?" Charlie asks.

Linc—*and what kind of name is "Linc"?*—laughs. "No, man. I've been so busy."

"That sucks!"

"It's the life of an adult." Linc laughs again, and I find myself smiling. His laugh is deep and throaty.

Jesus, he's pretty. I want to rub myself on him. *Ack.* What the hell is wrong with me?

Clearing my throat, I ask, "I take it you two know each other?"

Everyone looks at me, but Phillip's smile grabs my attention. "This is my buddy, Lincoln Scott. We went to school together. The boys have met him a few times."

"Oh," I say simply. I don't miss the way that Lincoln is looking at me. I may have been out of the game for a very long time, but I know when a man likes what he sees. Unfortunately, I know that because I watched my husband look at other women.

He steps toward me, and I find I'm holding my breath. He holds out his hand, his eyes dancing with mine. "Hi. I'm Lincoln."

"Oh." I take his hand with every intention to shake it quickly and be done with it, but apparently he has a different plan. Within seconds, his hand swallows mine and holds it tightly as his eyes burn into mine. Heat runs up my arms, my breath catches, and I swear I feel like I am the one who ran into duct tape and fell to my death.

I blink. He grins.

Riana claps her hands together. "So, I found your replacement for a nanny."

The spell broken, I pull my hand from his quickly, begging my body to behave. I try to ignore Hotty McHot and pull my brows up. "What? How?"

She just grins, and even with the shit day I've had, I can't help but smile. She is glowing and beautiful with her dark-blond bob and thick yellow glasses. I've always admired her style. I'm just plain, but she's always been intriguing. When I was pregnant, I looked like a cow, but she is stunning. I can't wait to meet my little niece. I envy Riana, and while I know it's wrong, I hope I always envy her. Because that would mean she'd always be happy. I want that for her. Always.

"The family this person was with just moved three months ago," she says. "He comes with great credentials, and we know him really well."

My brows come together in confusion. "Excuse me. *Him?*"

"Yeah. Lincoln," she says, hooking her thumb to him. "The manny."

My furrow digs deeper into my forehead, but I don't miss the pure excitement on my children's faces.

"No way!" Charlie exclaims.

I point to the guy I was just ogling ten seconds ago and almost had a coronary touching. "Him?"

Lincoln's grin pulls at his lips. "Me."

I fumble on my words. "But, but...you're a man."

Everyone laughs except me.

"Good observation. I am."

Oh, a smartass. Wonderful.

Elliot is hopping on his heels. "Mom, this would be so cool. Lincoln is so much fun."

I don't want fun. I want someone who can throw the hammer down! Someone to keep them alive and get them from point A to point B. Fun is the last thing I need. And a man to take care of my children? That just isn't what I want. I want someone nurturing—nice but hard—and someone who doesn't awaken my wild loins.

*My wild loins! Wow.*

Leaning toward me, Phillip whispers, "Change your

face before Riana starts yelling."

I didn't even realize I was making a face until I glance back at Riana. She is, of course, glaring and very annoyed. I clear my throat and ask, "Can I talk to you in the kitchen?"

She squints before leaning down to kiss Louis's head. "Yeah, come on."

I turn and notice Lincoln watching me. His eyes are intent on mine, his gray gaze so deep I swear it's as if he is challenging me. As if he is daring me not to hire him! I don't know this man from Adam, so why the hell would I hire him? He doesn't know what I want to talk to my sister about. Why do I care about what he thinks of me? Why do I like the way his lips quirk?

Oh, yeah, he's trouble.

My annoyance runs deep as we reach the kitchen. I shake my head as I move around the island, and I look up to see Riana crossing her arms across her chest, gently resting them on her growing stomach.

"Riana—"

"What? He's great," she says, cutting me off. "Honestly, Vera, he is amazing. He was with his last family for six years, and they love him. I had him forward all his credentials and letters of recommendation to you. You won't find anyone else like him."

"Well, no, 'cause he's a man!"

"Just open your computer and read through his stuff. I don't know why the fact that he has a cock swinging between his legs matters, but for real, drop it."

It matters because I wouldn't mind seeing said cock.

*This story continues in*
*Misadventures with a Manny!*

# ACKNOWLEDGMENTS

Thank you to the entire team at Waterhouse Press. Your help and support from start to finish of Speed Demon meant the world to me. This book wouldn't have been possible without your dedication and hard work.

Jeanne – Thank you for challenging me. Even though you liked the first version, I was over the moon you loved the second.

# MORE MISADVENTURES